ℳ for ℳisfit

Sarika Pandit lives in Mumbai but zips out of the city whenever pangs of wanderlust strike. When she is not travelling, she splits her time writing and working as a market research professional. Her travel articles have featured in publications such as *The Times of India*, *National Geographic Traveller*, *Mint*, *The Pioneer*, *Deccan Herald* and *Femina*.

Her first book, *Bucket List of a Traveloholic*, a travelogue, was published in 2014.

M for Misfit

SARIKA PANDIT

RUPA

Published by
Rupa Publications India Pvt. Ltd 2014
7/16, Ansari Road, Daryaganj
New Delhi 110002

Sales centres:
Allahabad Bengaluru Chennai
Hyderabad Jaipur Kathmandu
Kolkata Mumbai

ISBN: 978-81-291-3544-5

First impression 2014

10 9 8 7 6 5 4 3 2 1

The moral right of the author has been asserted.

Typeset in Electra LT Regular by SÜRYA, New Delhi

To,
Silver Linings

1

'Visitor?' the guard at the security gate asked.

'No,' I panted, glancing at my watch. 8.15 a.m. Phew! Not late. Thank God.

'I will need to see your employment ID please,' he said.

I looked up and blinked at him. 'I don't have one,' I croaked. 'You see, I'm, er, new here...'

'Ah!' he said in comprehension, 'first day on the job?'

I nodded. Behind him, rose an intimidating glass hulk of a building, the letters 'J&K Ltd.' mounted on it.

I stared at it, swallowing hard. 'First day on any job ever,' I whispered.

The Security Guard looked at me for a moment, then gave me a sympathetic nod. He thrust a pink card into my hands, the words 'Temporary Pass' stamped on it. Mouthing thanks, I stuffed the card into my trouser pocket and turned to walk towards the building. I had barely taken a couple of steps when I stopped abruptly. The image of a lamb walking into a slaughterhouse had just flashed before my eyes in vivid detail. I, Zoey Verma, (Management Trainee and First-time Jobber), was the dumb lamb in that scenario, and J&K Pvt. Ltd. (To-be Employer and Fridge Manufacturing Giant), was the proverbial slaughter-house of gore.

I should have been excited. My first day on the job, after all.

But I wasn't. I was afraid. Very afraid. My heart was beating so hard I expected it to explode right out of my chest. I took a deep breath and shuffled forward, trying hard to look confident but two steps later, I was pretty sure that I was back to looking scared shitless. *It's not too late*, a voice in my head whispered. *You can still turn and run.* I blinked, tentatively hovering near the entrance. Should I? Should I run? I shifted my weight from one leg to the other, then slowly began to turn back.

No! another voice shrilled in my head. *No running! Come on, woman. Get a grip. You can do this. You know you can.* If the second voice in my head belonged to 'Ideal Zoey' (the Zoey whom I imagined as the confident, grab-the-bull-by-the-horns, 'Indra-Nooyi' type, destined for big things), then the first voice belonged to, well, the 'Real Zoey' (the Zoey who preferred to bury her head in the sand like an ostrich and avoid all things, big or otherwise).

I turned back and was still gaping at the building and chewing my thumbnail, when Ideal Zoey snapped. *Get a move inside now! I mean, isn't this the moment you spent the last two years of your life at B-School for?*

'Er, right,' I mumbled, dragging my right leg forward.

Real Zoey snorted. *I thought you spent the last two years in B-School mastering the art of class-bunking and beer-guzzling...*

I faltered, gulped, then took a step back.

Don't listen to her, Ideal Zoey thundered. *Ok, so you may have bunked the occasional class (or, erm, more) and you may have guzzled beer enough to fill the Grand Canyon with, but you also cleared your Marketing exams. So, you are not an idiot!*

'Erm, right,' I agreed and placed my right foot forward again. I *did* pass my Marketing exams. I can't be a complete idiot. From the corner of my eye, I could see the Security

Guard watching me warily as if I was a borderline mental case. I couldn't blame him. In the last ten seconds, I had put my right leg in, put my right leg out, put my right leg in again, and pretty much shaken it all about.

OK Miss Marketing Wiz, Real Zoey mocked, *Let's see if you can answer this then—what are the four quadrants in the BCG matrix?*

My left foot hung above the ground. 'Er,' I scratched my head, '...er, I know the answer, it's erm, wait, give me a second, let me think...' I bashed my forehead with my fist. 'It's...it's...'

Hah! You don't know the answer, Real Zoey smirked. *Face it, woman. You have no idea what you are doing here or how you even got here. You are CLUELESS. You may as well go home and crawl back into bed where you belong.*

'Oh God! Oh God! You are right. I am clueless!' My throat tightened. Suddenly I was having trouble breathing. I massaged my heart and took five steps back, the crook of my knees colliding against something hard. A bench. I slumped onto it, and wiped my brow. It was cold and sweaty. Leaning forward, I buried my head in my hands. How had I gotten here? *How? How? How?* Even as that question kept looping around in my head, I knew the answer. I was here because of that interview. *That damned interview.*

My mind flashed back six months, to the most god-awful nerve-wracking seven days of my whole life—the dreaded B-School Placement Week. It was Day 3, and I had spent the last fifty-two hours hopping around from one interview to another, expressing an ardent desire to sell everything from soaps to trucks, but without much luck. By the time I was summoned for the J&K interview, I was drained, and nearing physical collapse. I had reached a point where I no longer cared whether I nailed the interview or not. All I wanted to do was to jump into the nearest bed and sleep for the next hundred years.

Somehow I had managed to reach the lobby outside the interview room where I sat blearily observing the remaining five sorry batchmates who—like me—hadn't managed to get placed yet. Batch mate No. 1 was gnawing off his tie. Batch mates 2 to 5 looked like they hadn't had a bowel movement in months. I, on the other hand, sat there, expressionless and still, like a block of wood, too comatose to care.

Just then I heard someone thump down on the seat next to me. I turned to meet a pair of protruding eyes in a thin, pointy face. Ugh! It was The Schmoozer. Claim to fame: amongst the top ten rankers of the batch. Core competency: schmoozing. Special achievements: the schmoozing of every rump on the campus, notable amongst them: the Dean and the Head of Marketing.

He nodded at me, then turned to scrutinize the others in the room.

'The look of desperation,' he chuckled, shaking his head. I clamped my lips together. God, he was annoying! And so damn smug. Didn't he have anything better to do than to sit here and gloat? I looked at his head and wondered how it would feel to bowl a brick at it.

'What are you doing here?' I lashed out at him, my irritation running high.

He turned to me slowly, running a hand through stiff, over-gelled hair. 'Same as you. Waiting for the interview.'

My eyes widened. '*You mean you haven't gotten placed yet?!*'

'I wouldn't say that exactly,' he said, clearing his throat, 'I mean, I got several offers…but you know, I deliberately didn't accept any of them. You see, I wanted to apply to J&K…it's a really good company…so well known…'

The liar! my mind yowled in a delayed flash of genius. Who was he kidding? J&K—*and well known?* Bah! I hadn't even been aware of its existence until three hours ago. And I was willing to bet that neither had he. Face it Schmoozer, you are here because no company wanted you. You are a placement reject. Just like me! Hah!

Suddenly, I was feeling positive. Despite The Schmoozer's 6-plus-CGPA and my, ahem, 4-minus-CGPA—at this point he and I were on an equal footing. That changed everything. It was as if a shot of adrenaline had been pumped into my arm. I escalated from feeling numb and jaded to, now, nervous and jittery all over again, a surge of nausea rising up my gut. It was official. I was back—full throttle—into interview mode. Hurrah!

Ten minutes later, while The Schmoozer was still waxing lyrical about the many virtues of J&K, a slightly harried looking junior staff popped into the lobby. 'Zoey Verma?' he asked, looking around the room. 'Yes, that's me,' I declared brightly, bounding up. 'This way please,' he said, leading me through a corridor towards the interview room. I stole a glimpse at my reflection in one of the glass windows along the way, and almost screamed. My hair was sticking up like the Eiffel Tower. *Bugger*, I cursed, quickly beating it down to a more acceptable shape, but a second later it bounced back to original position and waved at me cheerfully from the next window.

'All the best,' my escort whispered as we stopped outside a door. I gave him a tight nod, and ignoring the frizz fest on my head, pushed the door open and marched in.

At the head of the rectangular glass table, sat a youngish woman with thick glasses and poorly managed facial hair. My eyes rested on the fuzz above her lips for a fraction of a second before darting to the elderly man sitting two seats away. I stopped short—mid-stride—as my gaze zeroed in on his balding head. This was no proud balding head. This was a balding head that was cowering in shame, heroically covered by long tufts of grey hair coiled from above the right ear all the way across to below the left ear. I gaped at it in fascination. Suddenly, my own shabby-Monica-Geller-in-humid-Barbados-like appearance didn't bother me as much.

Creepy Hairdo was now standing up and stretching his hand out to me. I reluctantly tore my eyes away from his head, and in the spurt of my newfound confidence, gave him a mother-of-all-firm-handshakes. Then I looked him in the eye and flashed him my broadest 'you're-going-to-love-me' smile. Creepy Hairdo blinked. He didn't know what had hit him. A moment later, he coughed and cleared his throat. 'Please sit down,' he muttered, lowering himself in his chair.

I took my seat, and tilted my head forward expectantly.

He pushed what looked like my CV towards Glasses-n-Whiskers who picked it up from the table, gave its contents a perfunctory glance and looked up at me. 'Why don't you tell me a bit about yourself?' she asked.

'Sure,' I said eagerly. I opened my mouth wide and launched into a year-by-year account of my entire academic history, starting from school through to Junior college, to Senior college and ending with B-School. I had been blathering on for eight minutes when I realized that behind her thick lenses, Glasses-n-Whiskers' eyes had glazed over. I stopped suddenly to look at Creepy Hairdo. He seemed engrossed in studying the sole of his leather shoe.

'Anyway, THAT'S ALL,' I wrapped up my speech, almost shouting.

Glasses-n-Whiskers flinched, her eyes clearing up. Ah good,

she was back in the land of the living. 'Er, yes, right' she said, blinking several times. Then she adjusted her spectacles and asked, 'If you were to think of yourself as an animal, which animal would you be?'

It was my turn to blink madly. 'I'm sorry. What was the question again?' I filed a mental post-it for later use: *Get ears cleaned.*

'If you had the power to become an animal, which animal would you be?' Glasses-n-Whiskers repeated patiently.

Hell. I tore my mental post-it, then glanced at Creepy Hairdo, searching his face for a reaction. Much help his face was! It looked about as deadpan as Arnold Sh-what's-his-name's-mug. I checked back at Glasses-n-Whiskers. She looked expectant and was now leaning forward, chin upon clasped hands.

It took another minute, perhaps two, for my brain to register the fact that an answer to *that* question was expected. My mind jolted out of its stupor and started racing. *Which animal should I be? How the hell should I know?* Suddenly, an image blazed into my head. A little Chihuahua peeping out of Paris Hilton's pink basket, wearing a pink Tee Shirt with 'BFF' written on it. Oooh! If only I could be that Chihuahua. I'd be getting my fur shampooed and primed right now, instead of mouldering away out here.

'Well?' Glasses-n-Whiskers broke into my blissful reverie. She was now tapping a pencil impatiently on the table.

'Tiger,' I blurted out, in a voice of epiphany. Something told me that Miss Hilton's Chihuahua would not go down well with her.

'Hmm,' she nodded and furiously scribbled something on my CV.

'And if you were to think of yourself as a bird, which bird would you be?'

Oh, for heaven's *sake!* What *was* J&K Ltd.? The local zoo? I sighed inwardly. Beggars couldn't be choosers. Even working in a zoo was a better alternative to being jobless. Alright, let's see. Pigeon? Nah. Too dumb. Peacock? Nah. Too vain. Sparrow? Nah. Too twittery. What other birds were there? Aha…wait… 'Eagle!' I gasped in a flash of inspiration. 'I'd…I'd want to be an eagle.'

Glasses-n-Whiskers beamed and nodded. I beamed right back. Yay! Ten points to Zoey!

It was Creepy Hairdo's turn to ask the next question. 'So why do you want to join J&K?'

Because I am desperate. Because I need a job. Any damn job. 'Well, you see, I want to join J&K because…' I paused. He waited. I waited, too, for a stroke of genius. It didn't come. *Come on*, Zoey. *Think.* My forehead knotted. I could almost feel my head hurt. Wait, what was it about J&K that The Schmoozer had droned on about? Something about it being well known…established…good portfolio of products…

I quickly spewed out those words in the exact same order.

'Hmmm,' Creepy Hairdo nodded, stroking his chin. This is fun, I thought, beginning to enjoy myself. It's almost as if I'm on a Quiz show. Bring it on, Derek O'Brien.

Derek's next question was: 'And why should we hire you?'

Hah! The question for which I had a thoroughly well rehearsed recipe.

Recipe for *Why I Should Be Hired*: First, throw in some gassy adjectives, e.g., Determined, Committed, Detail-oriented, Motivated. Then add a few farty nouns, e.g., Team Player, Perfectionist, Micro-Manager, Strategist. Next, chop in a bunch of airy phrases, e.g., 'Like to take initiative', 'Always up for a challenge', 'Have unquenchable thirst for knowledge' etcetera. Garnish the brewing concoction with a handful of verbs, some vigorous gesticulation, and one or two random references to business stuff that I knew nothing about and, *Voila! One impeccable delivery of why I am God's Gift to every recruiter on the planet.*

'Besides, I am quite fascinated by the prospect of selling batteries,' I bunged in at the end for good measure. It was all a big fat lie of course, but I was on a bullshitting roll and I was unstoppable. A twinge of guilt niggled its way into my consciousness. I quickly filed Post-it No. 2 for when I was done with the interview: *Have a chat with God.* I hoped to be able to convince Him that I wasn't really lying; I was merely airbrushing my image.

'Fridges,' I heard Creepy Hairdo say.

'Eh?'

'J&K is in the business of selling fridges, not batteries,' he said neutrally.

'Er, of c-course,' I stuttered, feeling my face burn. 'Fridges, yes, yes. Er, those big things that, er, cool.' My voice cracked. I cleared my throat, 'I'm quite fascinated by them, er, fridges, that is. Er, quite fascinated.'

There was a long pause. Creepy Hairdo's eyebrows shot up. I clenched my fist and managed a feeble smile.

'And you'd be comfortable doing a sales job?' he asked, his eyes boring into my head.

Hahaha. You're joking, right? I couldn't peddle an igloo to an Eskimo if I tried. 'Yes.'

'And you'd be comfortable with a posting in any part of the country?'

If by any part of the country, you mean Mumbai and Mumbai alone. 'Yes.'

'And you're comfortable driving a two-wheeler?'

What? No! I can't even ride a tricycle without losing my balance. 'Yes.'

Frankly, with all that lying, I was rather surprised that my nose hadn't grown a mile long and crashed right through his head. I espied Glasses-n-Whiskers still making copious notes.

'Right then,' Creepy Hairdo suddenly boomed. 'That'll be all. Thank you.'

I nodded and got up. He heaved up, adjusted his tie and was about to offer me his large, knotty right hand again, but at the last minute changed his mind. I grabbed it nonetheless, shook it so vigorously that one major tuft of his hair sprang up, then flashed him and Glasses-n-Whiskers a 'you'd-be-mad-not-to-hire-me' grin and waltzed out of the room.

I suppose all that pathological lying...er...*airbrushing* must have paid off because a few days later, on the day of graduation, I received my first (and only) offer letter, scrawled on a big, bold J&K letter-head. I had been ecstatic and had twirled around with joy all over the campus. Not because in the days following the interview I had uncovered — in the very depths of my heart — a burning fascination for fridges. Trust me, I had not. (I still regarded fridges with the same fondness as Dracula regards sunshine.) But because, I, Zoey Verma, Third-Ranker-from-Bottom and Virtually-Unemployable, had managed to land a job! My folks were thrilled too. My dad — because his only daughter was the first MBA grad in his family, (er, he needn't know that I was Third-Ranker-from-Bottom) and my mom — because she could now freely do what I knew she had been itching to do ever since I had turned twenty one: scout for prospective grooms.

My initial euphoria, however, soon lay on the ground, dead. In its place, there lurked severe contractions of terror. That, and a strong feeling of foreboding. Something told me that if I walked into the J&K building, they would discover that I knew shit-about-shit and that I was 'Sales-and-Marketing' challenged. I had a sudden, scary apparition of Creepy Hairdo, chasing me with a stick (his long tufts of hair flapping wildly around), hollering 'Fraud! Fraud!'

My first day at work. Me—nervous as hell—sitting on a bench outside the gate, counselling myself. *Oh for God's sake. It's just a job. How hard can it be to sell fridges? It's not as if you have to go in there and find a cure for cancer.* 'Erm, right' I mumbled, straightening up on the bench; until I realised that in fact I'd *rather* find a cure for cancer than face what awaited me inside J&K. Deflated, I promptly sagged back. *God, if only I hadn't lied at that damned interview.* I had a nagging suspicion that all those answers of mine would eventually come back to bite me in the face.

I peeked at my watch. 8.25 a.m. If I didn't enter the building within the next five minutes, I would be certifiably late. There was now a rush at the security gate as hordes of bright-eyed employees clad in various shades of grey stood in line to swipe their cards, looking like they couldn't wait to charge in. I wondered if it was because they were having ardent flings with J&K's fridges. Ah, well, okay, that might be a little extreme, but they did all look like they had a sense of purpose, like they knew where they were headed, like working in J&K was their grand calling in life. I felt a stab of envy. From where I sat, I could suddenly see the world divided into two groups of people, Those-Who-Knew-Their-Calling-In-Life and Those-Who-Didn't. And I was definitely leading the pack in the latter category.

Career cluelessness and I had lived together since the creation of time, a bit like 'Tom and Jerry' or 'Batman and Robin'. In Class II of primary school, when Mrs Furtado had asked us what we had wanted to be when we grew up, and when all the other children—like a bunch of precocious suckers—had answered pat, 'Doctors' and 'Miss Indias' etcetera, I had simply sat there and gawked at her like a mute retard.

Ever since, I have hated that question; the question which, unfortunately, everyone simply loves to ask. My tactics to volley it and its various forms have varied over the years. Let me illustrate my point...

<u>At age 10</u>
Some random relative: 'So Zoey, your cousin wants to be a singer when she grows up. What do you want to be?'
(Tactic 1: Change the subject)
Me: 'Uncle, why do you and aunty not sleep in the same room?'

<u>At age 13</u>
Another random relative: 'So have you decided what you want to do with your life?'
(Tactic 2: Rebel)
Me: 'Either a bartender or a pole dancer. It's a tough choice. But don't worry, I'm planning to flip a coin.'

<u>At age 14</u>
A certain teacher: 'Have you thought about what you want to do after Class X?'
(Tactic 3: Philosophise)
Me: 'Do I need to? Does it matter? What's the point of it, anyway? In the long run we are all dead...'

<u>At age 15</u>

My worried parents: 'Zoey, by now you must have decided what you want to become...?'

(Tactic 4: Use Process of Elimination)

Me: 'Of course. Not a Doctor. Not a Chartered Accountant. Not a...'

<u>At age 16</u>

My worried parents again: 'If you don't want to be a Doctor or a Chartered Accountant, how about becoming an Engineer?'

(Tactic 5: Go with the flow)

Me: 'Umm. Ok.'

You get the drift, right? Even my doing an MBA had little to do with mastering business administration, and more to do with:

A) Hooking a cute, brainy hunk (top priority) and

B) Securing a fancy, fat-paying job

Unfortunately, at the end of two years in B-School, all I had to show for myself was a nasty break-up (we'll get to that later) and the knowledge that the world didn't really need another MBA. And, okay, so I have a job. But let me assure you, fat-paying it certainly isn't. And *fancy?* Erm, *hello?* Have you *seen* J&K's fridges?

8.28 a.m. The rush at the gate had receded. An elderly gentleman was now swiping his card. I wondered how old he was. Nearing sixty, I guessed. Close to retirement age. The lucky dude. His professional life was almost over and he was probably looking forward to a future of bumming around and drinking beer—I mean I couldn't think of a better life at this point. I wanted to be him. Come to think of it, I wanted to be anyone other than me at that moment. Even the Security Guard at the gate, who was now regarding me with renewed interest, would do just fine. I stole a look at my watch again. *Time's a slippin', girl*, it seemed to warn. Suddenly I knew that I had two choices—Choice No. 1: Sit on this bench until I sprouted fungus. (Very very tempting.) Or, Choice no. 2: Get up and get to it.

I snapped to attention pronto, and yanked my bag onto my lap; it was critical to first bribe myself into a more heroic mood, before doing any *getting up and getting to it*. So, in the absence of Kamikaze shots or Long Island Iced Teas, I quickly rummaged through my bag for my Oreo biscuit and bit into it with a savage *crunch*. Then, I vaulted from my seat and clapped my hands. 'Come on woman, let's get this show on the road!' I boldly declared, almost immediately feeling the onset of diarrhoea.

Ideal Zoey nodded wisely, '*Atta girl!*'

2

Five hours into my first day and my system was in a state of shock. I had just heard three back-to-back presentations tell me that a refrigerator was not just *that thing that cooled*. Apparently it had all sorts of parts and pieces. Pumps. Motors. Filters. And a whole bunch of other stuff. Who the hell knew? And quite frankly, who the hell cared? Okay, so I understand that at some point I might have to sell one, but did I really need to know the function of a compressor? I mean, what was J&K expecting us to do? Sell fridges and *repair* them too?

I looked around the conference room. Ten other Management Trainees from different institutes sat huddled around a circular table. I slowly studied each of their faces. Trainee No. 1: Shiny-Faced. Spellbound. Perched almost off the chair, trying to crane a closer look at the slide on the screen. (Trainee No. 2: Me. Bleary eyed. Bored stiff. Jaw aching from having to smother at least forty yawns in the last one hour). Trainees 3 till 7: Same stance as Trainee No. 1.

Trainee No. 8: Lara Krishnan. A girl from my B-School. Nostrils flared, cheeks inflated, she was, at that moment, attempting to stifle a great, big, fat yawn; but not having had as much practice as I'd had, was not quite able to manage it. I caught her eye and grinned. She grinned back, then curled her lip at the presenter, who was still jawing on about god-knows-what-part of a fridge.

Thank God for Lara. She was like an oasis in a desert of bright-eyed trainees who looked like they were on crack. Lara had majored in Finance, had even aced Accounting, but unfortunately for her, very few Finance companies had visited the campus during the placement week, what with recession and all of that. And so, she had joined J&K because the only thing worse than a Sales/Marketing job in her book, was no job at all.

In B-School, the two of us had revolved along completely different orbits. While I had spent my time fending off boring lectures on campus, she—the recipient of Fantastic Looks— had spent her time fending off drooling guys. Next to her satin-smooth hair and petite frame, I (with my frizzy hair and 5-feet-9-inch frame) had always felt a bit like a giraffe plugged into an electric socket. But despite our limited interaction, I had always thought that she was nice-ish and without airs.

I shifted my attention to Trainee No. 9: Another one of my B-School batchmates. I called him 'The Beaver' because he reminded me of one, with his painfully eager face and his zealously shining eyes. When we had got our offer letters, The Beaver had wanted to join *two whole months* before the scheduled date. 'That way we'll have an advantage over the other trainees,' he had said. Lara had instantly vetoed his idea and flung him such a dirty look that he had quaked in his shoes for a whole minute and a half. It was then that I knew Lara and I would get on fabulously. I smiled at the memory, then let my eyes linger on The Beaver's face for a few minutes. He was practically twitching with excitement, as if he couldn't wait to run out and conquer the world of frost-free refrigerators.

Repelled, I tuned my attention to the last and final trainee— Trainee No. 10: The Schmoozer. I let out an involuntary shudder. Just my rotten luck that he had made it through to J&K as well. God, he made my blood boil—with his cocky looks and intelligent nods, as if everything that the presenter was vomiting out made perfect sense to him. Each time I looked at his face I had to squelch the urge to lean over and sock his jaw, just as I was doing now. Holding down my hands tightly in my lap, I turned my attention back to the screen.

After a few minutes, I found myself summoning up all my energy to suppress my 41st yawn. It was 3 p.m. and my body was craving the nap it was so used to having at that hour. I turned wistfully to the window, wishing that I was back to the start of the three-month vacation post B-School. Three months spent eating, napping and being a stranger to grim reality. Three months of pure bliss. I suppose I should be thankful that we had these two weeks of induction at least, before being formally thrown into our jobs. God knows, my head hadn't stopped spinning since morning, and I needed some time to still it before rushing off to sell fridges.

A half hour and a much-needed tea break later (during which time Lara and I bitched non-stop about The Schmoozer), we scuttled back into the room for (thank God) our last session of the day: an address by the CEO. Everyone rushed to their seats and waited, breathless and agog, as if Brangelina and their brood were about to make an appearance. I had just shoved a biscuit—from the tray on the table—into my mouth, when the door silently opened.

In came a young, bespectacled man, followed by a much older one with a horrendous hairdo, a hairdo, which...*wait-a-minute! I had seen before.* I jerked up in my chair. The young man scurried to the laptop on the table, hurriedly uploaded a presentation, then slunk off into a corner while the older man took the centre-stage. 'Good evening all of you...' he began, clearing his throat. Well, well, well, I thought. So Creepy Hairdo was the CEO. Somehow, at the interview, I had pegged him as a lower-rung Marketing minion. Who would have thought that underneath that dodgy comb-over, sat a CEO's brain?

'Each of you should feel privileged to be a part of J&K,' Creepy Hairdo/The CEO was now saying. I listened for another few minutes—about just how privileged we should be feeling—before tuning out. The last three months of holidays had definitely shortened my already-short attention span. Folding my hands under my chin, I began pondering over my favourite daytime puzzler: Who is more beddable? George Clooney or Johnny Depp?

But soon, I decided to tune back into the present, just in case The CEO was talking Important Stuff. I needn't have bothered, because he was still talking fridge stuff. I happily tuned off again, this time settling on my second favourite daytime puzzler: Who is more husband material? Mr Darcy or Heathcliff? Even as I was trying to decide, a small part of my brain—the one that wasn't fantasizing about Colin Firth—registered the fact that all had suddenly gone mute. I slowly blinked and looked around. Every eye was pinned on me, including those of the CEO. My heart slammed to a halt.

'Is that right Ms Verma?' I heard the CEO ask. I panicked. Was what right? My mind scrambled. *Was what right, dammit???*

'Yes,' I bleated, the word tumbling forth without permission, having entirely bypassed my brain. The CEO frowned. *Shit.*

'Er, no...I meant, no,' I stuttered, feeling my face burn. His frown deepened. *Shit. Shit. Shit. Was it too late to ask what the damn question was?*

'What's it going to be,' The CEO asked in a quiet manner 'a yes or a no?'

I took a shuddering breath and decided to go with my first instinct. 'It's a y-yes.' It occurred to me that his question could very well have been 'Are you the biggest moron on earth?'

'Are you sure?' he asked, leaning against the wall, arms crossed, watchful.

That I was the biggest moron ever? 'Yes,' I mumbled resignedly. Let's face it, I was officially McMoron. Now could I slink off to kill myself?

The CEO gave me one last penetrating look, then nodded and continued with his address. I held on to the table and took a deep breath. My heart was still knocking around like a bass drum. *What the hell had just happened?* I looked to Lara for some hint. She sent me a comforting look. I emitted a weak half-smile in return. Against my better judgement, I moved my face towards The Schmoozer. He was smirking behind his hand. I bit my lip and picked up my glass of water. Fighting the urge to baptise him with it, I took a sip, then resolutely turned back to The CEO.

For the next twenty minutes, I sat on edge, desperately avoiding The CEO's gaze like I would the bubonic plague. It was only when he reached the last slide and asked, 'Any Questions?' that I began to breathe normally. A hand swiftly went up. I groaned inwardly. Shiny-Faced-Trainee No. 1 raising her hand. *Again.* How did she do it? I mean, here she was asking her 116th intelligent-sounding question of the day, while I had walked for miles in my head without meeting a single one. 'Good question,' The CEO beamed, after hearing her out. Shiny-Faced-Trainee No. 1 nearly keeled over with joy, while I glowered darkly. What *was she?* A member of some secret

Desperate Class Participation cult that convened every week to discuss *fridges?*

God, I should have stayed in bed today.

Fifteen minutes later, the session was finally over. I took my bag and waited for Lara at the door. 'Phew,' she said as she hiked towards me. 'Day 1 of the rest of our lives.' I nodded bleakly. We were walking down the stairs, when The Beaver caught up with us. 'Wow, Zoey, that was a narrow escape with the CEO!'

'Hmmph!' I grunted.

'How could you have drifted off during his session?' he asked wonderingly. 'I mean he is the CEO!'

'I didn't drift off,' I said primly.

'Of course, you did. Your eyes had glazed over. Hell, Zoey, this isn't B-School, where it was okay to sit on the last bench and day dream…this is our job, our career…don't you realize how important it is to make a good impression…how important it is to…'

God, was he annoying or what. And even if there was a seed…oh alright, a Banyan tree…of truth, in what he was saying, his sermonizing from the self-righteous altar of his newfound Career Zen was really ticking me off.

'I didn't drift off,' I repeated staunchly, cutting in. 'I was just…'…long pause '…pondering.'

'Pondering about what?' The Beaver pestered.

'Fridges,' I retorted, then flicked my hair over my shoulder and purposefully sidestepped past him.

'So what were you really…ahem…pondering about?' Lara teased, when The Beaver was out of earshot. 'Oh, just stuff,' I mumbled pinkly. For a moment, I considered asking her what The CEO's question had been, but then decided not to. The last thing I wanted to do was to relive my trip to Humiliationville.

We were just nearing the gate on our way home, when I saw a group of men standing in a corner near the garage. They were furiously puffing away, listening with rapt attention to someone in their midst. I stretched up to get a better look. Ah, The CEO. He was addressing the group, between deeply drawn lungfuls of his cigarette. A couple of drags later, he chucked the stub to the ground, when — just as he was grinding it out with his shoe — a hand darted forward before his nose, madly waving about what looked like a pack of Marlboro Lights.

The CEO stilled the hand, pulled out a cigarette from the pack, then turned to thank the bloke to whom it belonged. I stopped in my tracks as his face came into view. Pointed. Protruding eyes. Brylcreemed hair. There was no mistaking it. The Schmoozer. Clearly, he had found a new butt to schmooze. I glared at him, my awe and repugnance thrashing about in equal measure. Quickly, before jabbing Lara's arm and pointing to him, I prayed that he would either: A) get run over by a bus or B) spontaneously self-combust.

'Why am I not surprised?' she grunted, grimacing. I shook my head and fought off a surge of despair. Here he was sneaking into the CEO's Smoking Club, armed with Marlboro Lights, while I had spent the last one hour sneaking out of The CEO's range of vision, armed with a twisted neck. For the nth time that day, I found myself wondering what the hell I was doing in J&K.

'Oh forget him,' Lara said, pulling my arm through hers. 'He was always a smooth operator.'

After an hour, I was standing glumly in the local train, my nose poised a few centimetres away from a greasy head. As the train lurched forward, a blast of coconut oil hit my nose. I swayed, then took one dizzy look at the rest of the passengers jammed against each other nose to armpit, and consoled myself that it could have been worse. At least I towered above them all. At least I could breathe—one of the upsides of being vertically unchallenged.

Destination in sight, I moved forward an inch towards the door, eager to step off. Despite its crowded trains, its manic traffic and its smell of decaying corpses, I had a gigantic soft spot for Mumbai. This was the city in which I had toddled around in diapers, played with Barbie and Ken, mooned over pimply school-boys and head-banged to heavy metal. And so, even though my folks had shifted to Pune in the last year due to my dad's bank job, the city still felt like home to me.

I acknowledged, guiltily, that I was thrilled to bits that they had been transferred. I was quite looking forward to renting my own flat, getting a roomie and spending my weekends shoe-shopping, pub-hopping and beer-quaffing. Just let me get my final posting here—please God, please.

Outside the station, I hailed an auto for Bandra, where I was staying temporarily with my aunt (my dad's sister). As the auto thrust forward, I couldn't help but think of Lara's words. *Day 1 of the rest of our lives*, she had said. The thought left me feeling twitchy and weepy. No more two-month summer holidays. No more month-long Diwali breaks. Only an endless sea of days spent holed up in cubicles, staring at Excel sheets and PowerPoint presentations, with NOTHING to look forward to in between, except, *oh-wait*, the *weekends!* Suddenly the weekend shone on the horizon like a beacon of hope. One day down. Sigh. Four more to go.

When I got home, my aunt was ensconced in the couch, watching an episode of *CID*, her favourite show. The characters (surrounded by tubes and bottles of multi-coloured liquids in what looked like a laboratory) were trying hard to look pensive as they discussed a clue to some murder. I collected my dinner and stood next to the couch, my eyes fixed on those shiny liquids. Blue. Green. Yellow. Red. Heck. There was enough colour in that lab to fill up a giant rainbow. 'Funny,' I turned to my aunt, 'I was a Chemistry student and I am pretty certain that no earthly laboratory looks anything like that.' No response. Her eyes were riveted to the screen. 'In fact,' I continued, 'I'm willing to bet that no laboratory in the universe looks anything like that.' 'Shhh,' she hissed, her eyes still fixated on the screen. With a huff, I reluctantly flopped down beside her with my plate.

Within five minutes, during a break, she hit Mute and turned to me. 'So how was your day?' she asked, smiling. A lump wedged itself in my throat. I longed to fling myself at her and howl on her shoulders about how miserable I was feeling. I longed to be hugged and tut-tutted and there-there'd over. But my aunt was allergic to emotional diarrhoea. Her husband had expired just a few years after her marriage, and she had stoically and single-handedly raised her two sons, my cousins, both of whom were now 'settled' in the U.S. I was pretty sure that if I did crumple up into a blubbering heap in front of her, she'd simply and matter-of-factly advise me to stop being such a wuss. So, I bit my lip instead, and said, 'It was alright.' She nodded, and then promptly turned back to the screen.

Shortly after, my mom called. 'How was your first day, beta?' her voice trilled down the phone.

'Good,' I replied. As with my aunt, howling on my mom's shoulder was not an option—for entirely different reasons, however. If my aunt avoided emotional outpourings like she would Ebola, my mom with her penchant for Meena Kumari like melodrama, embraced it with a vengeance. Telling her that I was moments away from a good sob would entail her immediate descent at my aunt's doorstep, rolling pin in hand, all set to lug me off to Pune.

'Oh, good,' she said, before happily wittering on about the show-offs in her kitty party group, the rising price of apples, and how her most favourite character in her most favourite serial had suddenly died, only to return as the evil twin.

'...oh, one more thing before I forget,' she said, her voice deceptively casual.

'Yes?'

'Yesterday, I created your matrimonial profile...'

A long pause. I realized that my mouth was open. Shut it. 'You. Did. What?' I punctuated slowly.

'Your profile, beta...I made it yesterday...'

I gripped my phone hard. 'How could you?' I hissed.

'Oh, it was very easy...I just logged in and wrote...'

'You WROTE?' I yelled. 'Wrote WHAT?'

'Shaant baba,' my mom crooned, unfazed by the rapidly rising decibel level of my voice. 'I wrote that you are a nice, gentle, homely girl who...'

'I am no such thing,' I spat out in horror. Clearly the airbrushing gene ran in the family.

'Oof...I know that. But so what? The important thing is that many boys have shown interest. I gave your phone number to one of them. He will be calling you soon.'

'You did WHAT???' I thundered. I was THIS close to losing it entirely.

'I gave him your number,' she said calmly, 'he is a nice boy.'

'How the hell do you know that he is a nice boy?' I snarled impatiently.

'Because I got his horoscope read,' she chirped.

'Pah!' I grunted. 'I'm just twenty-three, mom,' I grizzled through clenched teeth. 'I am NOT interested in getting married just yet'

'Yes, yes, I know, but there is no harm in starting the process. Besides, his profile is very nice.'

'Oh *really?*' I asked, my voice dripping with sarcasm. 'And what does it say?'

'It says that he likes family values...' I rolled my eyes.

'...and has a stable job...' Another eye-roll.

'...He sells insurance, beta. Such a stable boy.'

'*How* lovely!' I hissed, feeling anything but stable. 'You can't go around sharing my number with random males on the net, mom,' I cried with exasperation. 'The fellow could be completely mental. He could be a...'

'No, no,' she said in an injured tone. 'He is not mental. He is...' She droned on about his many virtues for three more minutes (during which time I lost the will to live), finishing with '...so you see he is a good boy...'

'Have to go, mom,' I broke in curtly, and cut the call. My mom had frequent crazy notions, but handing out my phone number to strange men was definitely the crowning glory. I fell on to my bed and wished that she had called on the landline. At least then I would have had the satisfaction of banging the receiver on her!

Later that night, when my aunt was asleep in her room, I tiptoed into the kitchen, opened the fridge and viewed it with eager new eyes. Nope. Still didn't find it fascinating. The only thing fascinating about the darn thing were the contents of its freezer. Two large tubs of watermelon ice cream. I decided right then that I would drown my post-traumatic stress into:

A) One or both of those tubs, along with

B) My dog-eared pages of *Pride and Prejudice*.

The next two weeks of induction were a blur of one pesky presentation after another. I was bored out of my blooming back teeth. The other trainees, however, were maintaining their aura of zeal. What did they run on, dammit? Electricity? Did they plug themselves overnight and wake up each morning pulsating with power?

To make matters worse, I was beginning to feel muzzy. Numbers were flying at me from all directions and were, now, dancing before my eyes. Doing the tango were Monthly Sales and Market Shares. Spinning the salsa were Sales Growths and Annual Turnovers. Often, between blinking madly at them and lunging for the biscuits on the table, I would doze off until I had to be nudged back into consciousness by Lara.

But that wasn't the truly worrying part. The truly worrying part was that some of those charts and graphs had inadvertently managed to seep into my brain, because I had begun dreaming of fridges. In my last dream, I had opened a door, walking into what I was sure was George Clooney's bedroom, only to realize that it was actually a J&K Single Door Frost Free Refrigerator. I'm not sure how long I spent in the company of frozen cabbages and wrinkly tomatoes, while freezing away to death myself, before waking up with a start.

Friday evening eventually arrived, bringing with it the last session of our induction schedule: a presentation by the National Sales Head. The room buzzed with a collective rumble of anxious undertones as we sat waiting for the man to arrive, a man who was not only:

A) Second in Command to the CEO, but was also

B) Reputed to break the spirits of grown men with his pinky finger alone.

Soon enough, the man himself swaggered in. I stared at his face—*in alarm*—as he moved to the head of the table. With thick eyebrows and a moustache the size of a bus, the man looked like a throwback in a 1980's Bollywood baddie. Perhaps, the only thing diluting his badass look, I realized almost with dismay, was the fact that his pants were yanked up all the way to his chin almost.

I caught The Schmoozer surreptitiously sneaking in, from what I was sure was his 961st 'Smoking/Shmoozing break'. I scowled. It was a wonder he hadn't smoked his insides to soot yet. Lara had not missed The Schmoozer's entrance either because she began doing a whole production of the song 'Smooth Operator' under her breath. Trying to suppress the rise of a giggle, I accidentally let out a snicker. The sound must have reached the Sales Head's ears because he cranked his neck and slung me a chilly glare, one that could have restored the Ice Age. My heart rate kicked up. I briefly considered having my voice box removed.

'If you want to survive in sales,' he suddenly boomed, his vision slowly sliding across the room, 'especially consumer durable sales, you have to be tough. You have to be aggressive. You have to have your eyes on the target. At all times.' He paused, then moved menacingly forward, his eyes trained on me. 'I don't have the patience for wimps…' He paused again, watching me turn red; then seeming satisfied, swept a glance across the other faces. 'If you are a wimp, rest assured, I shall eat you alive.' I swallowed hard and trembled. *Did he think I was a wimp?* Hell. I quickly squared my shoulders and tried hard to look non-wimpy. Not so easy, given as I was still trembling, rather wimpily I might add. Wimp-eater looked my way pointedly again, then turned his head to read the first slide of his presentation.

It was at that moment that an astonishing growl pierced through the silence. 'What was that?' his head whipped around. Crap! *That* was my stomach, trying to tell me that it had been one hour since its last biscuit. I slunk further down my chair, my face on fire. Not daring to look at the other trainees, who I'm sure were staring at me, I looked down at my fingers and prayed for death. Seconds flitted by. Nothing happened. When I finally dared to look up, Wimp-eater had turned back to his presentation. I loosened up and breathed easy again. Just then I felt Lara press something into my hand. I looked down to see a cream biscuit. Whispering a sheepish thanks under my breath, and still refusing to look at the other trainees, I shoved the biscuit into my mouth hoping that Wimp-eater didn't have an eye protruding out the back of his head.

Then I turned to take a look at his slide. A table of the monthly sales figures, of five Area Sales Managers from Chennai, stared back at me. 'Look at Basu,' Wimp-eater was pointing to the name at the top of the table. 'Now, he is what I'm talking about. He is what I call a performer. Look at the number of refrigerators he has been consistently selling.' We all looked with due amazement.

His finger slowly slid to the two names at the bottom of the table. Srinivas and Badri. 'And look at these two jokers,' he sneered. 'Single-digit sales in one month! Shameful!' Wimp-eater had now begun pacing the room back and forth like some caged animal. 'If they continue at this rate I am going to throw them out,' he barked. We all flinched. All except The Schmoozer, who looked resolutely smug. 'J-o-k-ers,' Wimp-eater repeated, stretching the word into four syllables of disgust.

Something slipped from a shelf inside of me and came crashing to the floor. I suspected it was my already-dying spirit.

The rest of Wimp-eater's session saw me sitting terrorized, watching him rally about and yell, while praying that my stomach had found the good sense to shut up. When his slot finally concluded, I nearly blanked out with relief.

That evening, in light of the facts that 1) Wimp-eater had threatened to eat alive every poor-performing wimp on the horizon and, 2) Despite my valiant attempts to look non-wimpy, his wimp radar had flashed straight at me: I decided to drown my sorrows in the company of Long Island Iced Teas and Lara.

'That Badri,' Lara howled, 'that Badri is me. I am he. I am Badri.' We were slouched in a pub not too far from office, nursing our third LITs each. Lara was hitting her chest like a maniac.

'No, no, I am Badri,' I wailed, slapping my glass on the table. 'I am Badri!'

'Alright fine,' she gave in gloomily, then downed half her glass. 'If you are Badri,' she hiccupped, 'I am Sssshhhinivas. Either way, we are going to be the two jokersrsh on dishplay neksht year.'

'If we are not thrown out before, that is,' I moaned, shutting out visions of being pronged with a fork by Wimp-eater.

'And that Schoozer...Shoosher...' Lara slurred, bonking her hand on the table, '...that loosher...did you see him? Did you *see* him? Panting after the S-shales Head with his Marlboro freakin Lights...!'

'Yeah...' I mumbled. 'Sneaky little rat...I hate him.' I picked up my glass and swirled it under my nose. I wasn't quite as sozzled as Lara was, but I was definitely beginning to feel light and cheery, until I remembered, all too soon, that I had *bugger all* to be light and cheery about. At the rate I was going, I was sure to get sacked within a month.

'Can I buy you two a drink?' I heard someone ask. I looked up to see a lanky, big-nosed chap, lowering over our table, smiling at Lara and practically frothing at the mouth.

'Bugger off!' Lara slurred. 'Can't you shee we're upsshet?' Big Nose flinched, then quickly did an about-turn and scuttled out of sight. A pause followed, then Lara turned to me and whispered, 'I hope they don't put us in ss-sshhales...I hope they put us in [hic] Marketing...in [hic] Mumbai.'

I nodded fervently. I *so* didn't want to be in Sales either. And, I *so* didn't want to report to Wimp-eater.

'We'll know on Monday,' she said.

Yep. Monday. The day of reckoning. The day when we will be informed of our projects and final postings.

'Fingers crossed,' I croaked, downing the last remnants of my LIT.

3

If the last week had slugged along at the pace of a Kolkata hand-rickshaw, then the weekend had whizzed by at the speed of a Concorde jet. All too soon, it was Monday morning again, and I was back in the premises of J&K. For the first time in my life, I was able to well and truly appreciate Einstein's Theory of Relativity.

The atmosphere in the HR conference room was thick with tension. Nails were being bitten, cuticles being chewed and pens nibbled. My own heart was beating so hard that I was surprised it hadn't leaped out on to the table. I patted it down and decided that it was time to have a quick one-on-one with God. Within five seconds I was making all sorts of irrational promises to Him:

- Will donate first paycheck to a good charity.
- Will watch every instalment of CID with aunt and not laugh at the multi-coloured laboratory.
- Will no longer think that fridges are hideously uncool, and will devote all weekends (and evenings) to reading truckloads of books on Fridge Stuff.

Just please, please, please give me a Marketing role in Mumbai.

'Showtime,' I heard Lara announce. My eyes flew open. Glasses-n-Whiskers had just walked into the room, carrying a

stack of envelopes in her arms. She stood at the head of the
table, thwacked the stack on it, then picked up the first letter
and called out a name. The Beaver jumped up and scurried
forward. In a few moments, she called out mine. My stomach
turned somersaults as I walked up to collect my envelope. With
shaking hands, I ripped it open, vaguely hearing Lara's name
being called out next.

Please let it be Marketing in Mumbai. Please let it be
Marketing in Mumbai. Please let it be Marketing in Mumbai.
Sales. In Delhi.

I felt sick. My head began swimming. I reeled back to my
seat, dropped down and tried to stop myself from throwing up.
Seconds later, I read the letter again, just in case my eyes had
played tricks on me. Nope. Still Sales. In Delhi. *This cannot be
happening.*

My eyes frantically swept across to Lara. She sat frozen, jaw
slack, mouth open. 'Lara' I whispered. No response. Her letter
lay open in her limp hands. I grabbed it and quickly ran
through its contents. Two words danced maddeningly before
my eyes. Sales. Chennai. Jeez. 'Lara,' I tried again, a moment
later, tapping her hand. She flinched, then turned her head in
slow motion. 'I. Am. So. Screwed,' she whispered. 'Me too,' I
echoed miserably. She looked quizzically at my letter. 'Sales.
Delhi,' I complained.

She grasped my hand urgently. 'What are we going to do?'

'I d-don't know,' I replied shakily, then groaned, 'God, I
wish I hadn't lied at that interview. I should have said Paris
Hilton's Chihuahua instead of tiger.'

'And I should have said Justin Timberlake's Labrador puppy
instead of horse,' Lara complained. 'I haven't even majored in
Sales. The only reason I took this job was because of the
goddamn recession. You know, I don't even...'

I didn't catch the rest of Lara's words because at that moment a fresh wave of nausea charged up my throat. Cramming my fist in my mouth, I bolted out of the room as if I had a Grade 4 tornado on my tail.

Minutes later, having successfully ejected the omelette that I had had for breakfast, I weaved back to the room.

'Are you alright?' Lara asked, alarmed. 'You've gone white.'

'I'm okay,' I lied miserably.

My eye was caught by The Schmoozer who, from a corner of the room, was euphorically shaking his fists in the air. Next to him, Shiny-Faced-Trainee No. 1 was beaming so broadly that it was a wonder her cheeks hadn't cracked.

'What are those two looking so happy about?' I growled, hunching in my chair.

'You don't want to know,' Lara said, then rushed on to tell me nevertheless. It turned out that the reason Shiny-Faced-Trainee No. 1 was exuding sunshine all over the place was because she had bagged the Mumbai Marketing role. *My* Mumbai Marketing role. I scowled. A big, fat worm of jealousy began to wriggle about in my stomach.

'Clearly, it pays to be a member of a secret cult,' Lara said, an eyebrow shooting up.

I nodded downcast. Oh, who was I kidding? Let's face it. In the last two weeks, Shiny-Faced-Trainee No. 1 had been a model of drive and initiative. I, on the other hand, had been a model of dim-wittedness and ineptitude. No wonder I was being shipped off to Delhi.

'What about The Schmoozer?' I asked, the next moment.

'He is going to be in Mumbai too.'

'Fabulous,' I said dully. 'Doing what?'

'No idea. He isn't telling.'

'Why not?'

Lara shrugged. I glanced again at The Schmoozer. He was now strutting around the room like James Bond on some top secret assignment. I, meanwhile, sat there, all shaken, like his bloody Martini.

I turned to Lara. 'Can I just whack him with his letter?'

'Not a good idea.'

'Strangle him with his tie?'

'Definitely a worse idea.'

'Life sucks,' I fussed, sinking back in my chair.

'Look at the bright side,' Lara remarked, her tone snide, 'it's going to end soon. Wimp-eater is planning to eat us alive, remember?'

Wimp-eater! Oh God! I had forgotten about the Wimp-eater! I buried my head in my hands and groaned, my obituary flashing before my eyes:

> Zoey Verma (23) is missing and presumed dead. Close friends believe that she was eaten alive by her boss due to extreme wimpy behaviour. Her burning desire for dismembering her colleague The Schmoozer, remains, sadly, unfulfilled.

That afternoon, all the sales trainees (including a trembling me) assembled in Wimp-eater's cabin for our project debrief. Facing me was The Beaver, who, I learnt, had got a posting in Kolkata. He looked enormously thrilled about it. His eyes were shining brighter than usual and he was gazing at Wimp-eater with breathless devotion. I half expected that he would throw himself at Wimp-eater's shoes and start kissing them avidly. Meanwhile, Wimp-eater was looking him up and down as if examining a bug. When it was my turn to get eyeballed, I sucked in my breath, stapled on a smile and prayed that my now near-empty stomach wouldn't choose that precise moment to let out its legendary growl.

Wimp-eater grasped his belt and yanked his pants up even higher (they now reached his moustache almost), then he turned and pointed to The Schmoozer, 'He will be in Mumbai doing a separate assignment while the rest of you jo…ahem…while the rest of you *trainees* will be in the branches doing a market mapping project before being assigned your sales territories.'

Something told me that *jo…ahem…*was code for jokers.

'As a part of this market mapping project,' he bellowed, 'in the next three months, the four of you will conduct a retail audit of all the durable outlets in your respective branches.' He paused, sidled a vague glance at his vibrating phone, then continued, 'There are about a thousand such outlets in each of your cities and the immediate areas around it. Your task is to go to each of them and record two things. One, all the brands of refrigerators stocked in that outlet and two, the number of units of each brand in that outlet.'

I glanced at Lara, my eyes goggling in alarm. One thousand outlets? Did he want us to physically go to *one thousand* outlets??? Was he nuts??? I squirmed in my seat until it wobbled.

'And mind you,' he continued, for some reason now wagging a finger at me, 'when I say a thousand outlets, I mean you have to go to *each and every* one of those thousand outlets. I don't care how far they are or in what corner of the city, it is your job to cover them all.' I cringed and tightened up under his probing gaze. A moment later, he swivelled around to face The Schmoozer. 'You have another project,' he said, his face lighting up. 'Come with me, we will discuss it over a smoke.' Then he stalked out of the cabin, The Schmoozer dogging his footsteps.

The Beaver looked on, thoroughly bewildered. Lara shook her head and sniggered in disgust. I sat there, rubbing my thudding heart.

In the next one week, I rushed around trying to organize my move to Delhi, while simultaneously battling bouts of panic. It didn't help that my mom had called up every night since I had dropped the Delhi bomb, and squawked hysterically into the phone between soap-opera like snuffles. 'You can't go to Delhi...Delhi is not safe...What sort of a company is this...How can they send a girl alone to Delhi...Quit your job...Come home *right now...*' Tempting though that was, the Ideal Zoey in my head absolutely forbade it. By Day 5, however, my mom's ranting seemed a little less frenzied, thanks to my dad who—in a rare display of 'Head of the Household' behaviour—had announced that I should go to Delhi, because apparently I needed 'toughening up'.

'I don't know why your father wants you to toughen up,' mom rebuked down the phone-line three days before my departure. 'You are 8 feet tall as it is...already you scare off half the boys...how much more tough does he want you to be?' I inhaled deeply. God, I thought, give me strength.

'And what about that nice boy,' she continued, 'that nice boy from the matrimonial site...the one to whom I gave your number...I spoke to his parents...such a good family...such a good boy...'

I rocked on my heels and counted to ten. Odds on forward, evens on backward.

'...the boy is based in Mumbai...and here you are running off to Delhi...I don't know why you have to run to Delhi...meet the boy before you leave...'

'I am not meeting any boy, mom,' I said testily, and before

she could get in another word, 'Have to go now, mom…I have stuff to do,' and hung up. Hanging up on my mom, I noted, was becoming a regular occurrence.

I did have stuff to do, you know. I wasn't lying. I even had a to-do list in hand.

To-do List:
1. Pack bags
2. Organize flight tickets
3. Organize guesthouse stay in Delhi
4. Get broker contacts
5. Meet best friend from college
6. Meet best friend from school
7. Visit astrologer
8. See dentist
9. …

I locked on to Item No. 7, and brooded on it awhile. Was it only a month ago that I had been a sceptic, scorning the 'science' of astrology? I shook my head sadly. I was no longer that person. In the course of the last thirty days, I had morphed into Fox Molder. I now wanted to believe. My personal universe was spinning out of control and I desperately needed some cosmic reassurance.

That evening, when no one was looking, I logged on to the internet, typed 'INDIA'S BEST ASTROLOGER' into Google, then leaned back in my chair. A zillion links flashed up on the screen. I blinked. *Bugger*. Was every other Indian the best astrologer in India? I clicked on the first result. This bird had to be the best of the best, right? A fluorescent green page opened with a mug shot of the astrologer (bearded, bald and rather benign-looking) along with a dozen reviews about how he had accurately predicted so-and-so's impending marriage and so-and-so's impending doom. I was wildly impressed.

At 7 p.m. the next day, I landed up, anxiously, at the astrologer's doorstep, and was greeted by a young, earnest looking man who claimed to be the astrologer's secretary.

'Masterji will be with you in some minutes,' he said, as he led me into the waiting room. I nodded, sat on an empty seat in the corner, and cast a look at the only other person in the room. A zit-faced, scrawny teenager with greasy hair and a fetish for his nails. What did he want to know from the astrologer, I mused. Whether he would flunk his Calculus paper? Whether he would ever get laid?

Twenty minutes went by. Zit-face, having painstakingly bitten off the last of his nails, had now moved to his next pastime. Picking on his pimples. He was on Pimple no. 5, when the secretary poked his head into the waiting room and beckoned him. Zit-face sprang up and meekly trotted off behind him. He looked nervous. Ten minutes later, he came out looking even more nervous. Hmm. So he was failing his Calculus exam, then. Or, was he never getting laid? Or worse, both?

It was my turn next. My tummy flipped excitedly as I followed the secretary to the Masterji's office. As soon as I entered, I received a shock.

What in hell? Upon the erstwhile bald and gleaming head of the Masterji, there now sat a big mop of suspiciously jet-black hair, sticking out in tufts. I stared at it, transfixed.

'Namaste,' I heard the Masterji say, from behind his desk.

'Namaste,' I croaked, still gawping at His Mop. Was it a wig or had he transplanted some of the hair from his over-populated chin? Either way, it did nothing for his face.

'Sit, sit,' Masterji said, pointing towards a chair facing him. I sat hesitantly, eyes glued to His Mop.

He opened his drawer and pulled out a book. 'Your date, time and place of birth?' he asked.

I told him. He began to squiggle up my horoscope chart, while I continued to inspect His Mop. Thoughts began to race in my head. It can't be a transplant. It has to be a wig. It looks like a separate entity; as if 'It' has a life of its own. 'It' looks dodgy. He looks dodgy. Should I scram? Should I...

'Aha, Kanya Rashi!' he suddenly exclaimed, breaking into my stream of thoughts.

'Kanya Rashi?' I echoed, temporarily side-tracked. Was that good or bad, I vaguely wondered.

He began to nod his head up and down.

That must mean good, I thought, relieved.

Then with gusto, he began nodding his head from left to right.

Or bad, I thought, plaintively.

Finally, he began nodding his head in a circular motion.

I gave up. Noddy here was beginning to test my patience. His Mop had caught my attention once again. I was amazed that It hadn't rolled off with all that vigorous nodding. Perhaps It wasn't a wig, after all. Perhaps It was a transplant.

A minute later, he spouted a gem. 'You are confused,' he declared.

It was my turn to nod.

'You are worried,' he said.

I nodded again.

'You have come to seek answers,' he said.

I nodded some more. This man was actually quite...er...good.

'Do you have any specific questions you would like to ask?' he enquired.

'What do the next twelve months of my life look like?' I asked eagerly.

'Hmm,' he said, stroking his beard. 'Your *Rahu dasha* is going on...'

Non-celestial language please. 'Meaning?' I asked him.

'I see a lot of changes in your life. Yes, a lot of changes,' he said, reaching up for His Mop, almost as if to see whether it was still intact. Aha, so It was a wig then?

'What sort of changes?' I asked.

'Some good and some bad,' he announced, rotating his head again. His Mop didn't move a millimetre. Transplant then?

'Oh?' I said, waiting for him to elaborate.

He didn't; he merely closed his eyes. Ten seconds more. No response. 'Erm, what kind of bad changes?' I cleared my throat and asked, wondering if he had gone off to sleep.

'Shhh,' he said, opening one eye to throw me a 'shut-up-you-dumb-kid-and-let-me-concentrate-because-the-universe-is-trying-to-tell-me-something' look. Then he closed his eye again. 'Beware of the next few months,' he eventually said, 'I see troubled waters.'

'Really?' I asked, a knot forming in the pit of my stomach.

'Yes, very troubled waters.' He repeated ominously.

I whispered a strangled, 'Oh.'

'But it will get better after a few months,' he said smugly.

I relaxed dramatically in relief.

'Will I still have a job a year from now?' I asked. 'No wait,' I rushed on, 'will I still have a job a month from now?'

He pulled out a calculator and scratched His Mop.

The superficial scratching didn't seem to help because his face scrunched into a grimace. Alright, I decided; if, in the next six minutes, His Mop doesn't slide off, than I shall declare 'It' a Transplant, else I shall declare 'It' a Wig.

Five minutes and several nods later, he said, 'It depends.'

'On what?' I asked him.

'On you,' he said, scratching His Mop a little more vigorously. 'It's up to you,' he repeated. Wig? Transplant? Wig? Transplant? Wig? Transp...

'That is all I can tell you,' he said, interrupting my thoughts, 'My next appointment is waiting.'

'Oh, ok.' I said, feeling deflated. I wasn't sure if I had got all my answers.

'That will be 1000,' he said.

One thousand! This bird, sure as hell, was the 'best' when it came to billing. I fumbled for my wallet in my bag, found it, pulled out a wad of notes and thrust it into his hands. Then I turned and headed for the door, but not before one last glimpse at His Mop. Still intact. Gotcha!!!

I spent the next twenty-four hours trying to make sense of the visit. I suppose the gist of it could be summarized as follows:

- I have Kanya Rashi. That is not necessarily good or bad.
- There are going to be lots of changes in my life in the next 12 months—some good, some bad.
- Troubled waters for the next few months, but things will get better after.
- I may or may not be employed one month from now.
- His Mop *is* a transplant.

My aunt came to drop me off at the airport on the departure D-Day. I gave her a bone-crushing hug; as if that was the last time I would see her before being flung to the gallows. I wanted to also hug the black-and-yellow auto in which we had travelled; as if that was the last time I would see a black-and-yellow auto before being flung into green-and-yellow CNG land.

Two hours, and I stood outside the Delhi airport. The ball of anxiety that had been growing in my stomach over the last few days was now the size of the Titanic. I hailed a cab and within the hour, landed at the doorstep of the company guesthouse. It was late evening and the place was empty except for an old caretaker who looked barely alive, and a middle-aged man sporting an enormous pot-belly.

I kept my luggage in my room, and walked into the hall for an early dinner. Pot-Belly was lounging on a couch watching a cricket match, and Caretaker was laying the dining table with plates and parathas. I pulled out a chair and had just plopped three of those parathas on my plate, when Pot-Belly hauled himself up from the couch and plunged into a chair next to me. A current of uneasiness swept through me. Without looking up, I bit into my paratha. A minute later, Pot-Belly cleared his throat. 'Hi,' he said. 'Hi,' I murmured, my mouth full.

He was, I learnt straight away, a Sales Manager of some non-fridge division of J&K. 'Where are you from?' he asked, looking me up and down, rather slimily. 'Mumbai,' I mumbled and continued chomping. 'You are a brave girl,' he wheezed, 'coming all the way to Delhi. And that too, *all by yourself.*' Instinct made my skin crawl. The hair on the nape of my neck lifted. I began wolfing down my parathas even more rapidly. As fast as I could, my gut griping from the paratha onrush, I got up, gave him a backward dismissive wave and ran out of the hall.

Back in my room, my door firmly secured, I pulled out my contact list of brokers. I had a few days to sort out my accommodation before starting work. I tried calling a couple of them, then realizing it was too late in the night, flung myself on my bed for some private bawling. I had squeezed out two tears, when someone tapped on my door. Wiping the tears off, I walked to the door and opened it tentatively. Pot-Belly leaned against the doorframe, his hands resting on his pot-belly. 'Hi,' he said, breathing heavily. A gust of whisky hit me, like a football in the face. I jerked back. 'I was just wondering if you would like to join me for a drink downstairs.' He paused, then let out a loud belch. I shrank bank in horror, almost tripping over my feet.

Thankfully, I managed to quickly regain my composure. 'No, thank you,' I said curtly, jamming the door on his face. Then supporting myself against the wall I slid down to the floor. Some more tears arrived; this time accompanied with snivelling. *Oh God! Oh God! Where the hell have I landed?* I must be dreaming. Soon I will wake up and realize that it's all only a crazed nightmare, and I'll find myself in my warm, cosy bed at home, snuggled under my warm, cosy bedspread. I sniffed, then pinched myself. Nope. No warm, cosy bed. Still drowning in my nightmare.

My cell phone buzzed on my bed. I blinked, then lunged forward to take a look. A text from Lara:

JUST GOT YELLED AT BY RUDE AUTO GUY WITH RAJNIKANT HAIR

I quickly texted back.

JUST GOT HIT ON BY SHADY SALES GUY WITH BOOZY BREATH

Lara's reply was swift:

YOU WIN!

The next morning, terrified by the prospect of another day in the company of Pot-Belly, I dived into flat-hunting with a vengeance. In the scorching heat, I trotted behind the broker from one uninhabitable flat to another. Apparently, my measly budget could only afford flats that looked like they had been in the eye of a hurricane. After five hours of running around in circles, I began to feel swimmy. Stars danced before my eyes and beads of sweat trickled down my face. I leaned against the wall of a building, bent double, and mopped my feverish brow. How on earth was I going to survive in sales if I couldn't survive a morning in the sun? My feet were paining, my head was drumming and there was a roaring sound in my ears.

I was about to give up and give in to tears, when the image of Pot-Belly scratching his paunch and wheezing in my face flared up before my eyes. I bounced up without any further ado, blinking madly. Within two seconds, I was bounding behind the broker like a gazelle.

Thankfully, soon after, I happened upon a flat close to my office, which just about managed to meet habitable standards. The landlord, a wiry, sixty-plus old man, waited in the hall as I inspected the other rooms. Satisfied, I traipsed back to ask him a few questions about the flat. Once it was all tied up, he cleared his throat and asked, 'Are you married?' I shook my head. A beat of silence, then he said, 'I have a son. Very handsome. Very tall. Has a good job. Drives a Toyota Corolla...'

I nodded benignly, wondering how this story was going to end.

'Why don't you give me your home address, beta? I will courier his photo to your parents.' Then he turned to the broker, 'Oye, Bluedart ka number hai kya?' I closed my eyes in pain. *That's all I needed. Grandpa, the Matchmaker.* I decided right then and there to give the flat a miss.

But later, at the guesthouse, when a lurking Pot-Belly gave me 1) a sleazy smile, accompanied with 2) a leery wink and 3) asked me what time I would join him for dinner, I raced to my room like a bullet, latched my door, dialled my broker's number and thundered, *'YES? HELLO!! I WILL TAKE THAT FLAT!'*

4

My first day at the branch office. I stood outside the cabin of my boss, the Delhi Branch Head, my heart drumming, trying to summon up the courage to knock at his door. Be calm, Zoey Verma, I told myself. Be confident. Banish all terror! Banish it, I say! Unfortunately, Terror gave me a slap in the face at that very moment as a loud roar pierced the air from within the cabin. 'Abbey saalon!!! Dhakkan ki fauj!!!' I dunked and nearly crapped in my pants. *Who the effing eff was that???*

'...Aise sales figures mujhe dene mein tum logon ko sharam nahin aati?!' the voice thundered. 'Uttar doonga ek ek ki!!!'

Hell, Damn and Eff. *Was that the Branch Head?* I shook. He sounded less like a Branch Head and more like a gun-toting don. Half expecting a gunshot to go off any second, I looked around wildly and had a flashing thought to fly out the window by way of escape. Sadly, blocking my exit was The Don's secretary who, at that moment, was nudging me forward towards the door. I took a shuddering breath and, heart racing even faster, tentatively knocked on the door.

'Come in,' I heard The Don order. I whispered a silent prayer, opened the door and walked in. At the head of a small table sat a man with a round face, a French beard and a horrendously big nose. The Don, I figured, nervously. Facing him across the table stood four stocky guys with sweaty faces and bloodshot eyes. They were all staring at me as if a chimpanzee had suddenly descended amongst them.

'What do you want?' The Don growled, scowling fiercely.

'Erm,' I tried to speak; no words came out. It was as if they were stuck in my throat like glue. 'Erm,' I tried again, clasping my hands together, 'I'm the n-new Management Trainee...'

The Don studied me, derisively, from top to bottom. 'So *you* are the *bakra* whom Head Office has sent to do that *faltu* project.' He turned to the four Area Sales Managers, eyes still on me, 'Is bakre ko bola hai Dilli ke saare outlets ko map karne ko.' The four ASMs started sniggering. I stared miserably at them, praying for the ground to open and suck me in.

'Sales kabhi kiya hai pehle?' The Don asked. I dumbly shook my head. 'Hai Bhagwaan!' he exhaled, then began muttering. 'Pata nahi yeh Head Office wale apne aap ko samajhte kya hain...kisi ko bhi recruit kar lete hain...'

I gaped at him, suddenly breathless. Two facts had simultaneously dawned on my traumatized self. Fact No. 1: The 'bakra' in question was me. Fact No. 2: Not only was I, apparently, a big joke, but so was my project. Suddenly, I had an overwhelming urge to eat ice cream until I conked out.

'Well?' he asked a few minutes later, after shooing off the four ASMs. 'So how are you going to go about this...this *project?*' He said project with as much distaste as one would reserve for a lizard. I stared at him, mute. *How the hell should I know how I would be doing this project? I mean, did I look like I could foretell the future?* 'Well?' he repeated impatiently. He was leaning forward, fixing me with a full-powered stare-down. 'Um, I-I'm not sure,' I whispered, ingesting a bit of bile. His brow furrowed with annoyance, then he seized a handful of his hair as if he wanted to pull it out in frustration. 'Mujhe hi kyon milte hain aise joker?!' he muttered under his breath.

I bit my lip, willing myself not to burst into tears. The Don stared angrily at the ceiling for some seconds, then leaned back in his chair and turned to me wearily. In a supremely patronizing tone, as if to some thickhead on a mental strike, he began explaining the sales structure. Each ASM, he said, was allocated one zone or territory in the city and serviced the distributor allocated to that zone. The distributor, in turn, supplied J&K fridges to all the durable dealers in that zone. He then explained that I would have to map the city, zone by zone, starting with South Delhi, for which I would need to take the help of the South Delhi ASM and distributor.

It all sounded like utter hell to me. I felt overwhelmed. I had no idea how I was going to manage. I was about to fling myself on the table and break into bitter tears, when The Don unexpectedly pushed his chair back and got up to indicate that the meeting was over. He turned out to be all of 5 feet 2 inches short; and had to crane his neck to look up at my face. I stared at him. So he wasn't just The Don; he was *Chhota* Don! I cowered near the door, feeling suddenly conspicuous. Chhota Don was now looking even more irked. He expanded his chest, as if that would help add a few inches to his frame. Unfortunately, it didn't. Agitated, he thumped his fists on his chest like Tarzan and roared, 'I will want a report every day about your progress! Every day, understand?!' I nodded dejectedly before he ordered, 'Go, I have work to do.' I timidly tottered out of the cabin.

For a minute, I stood stupefied outside the door, feeling as if I had just been pole-axed by a truck. Then I blinked and slowly looked around the hall, vaguely registering the fact that in comparison to the rich, sprawling Mumbai Head Office, the Delhi Branch looked like its poor, neglected cousin. Tired looking tables stood cramped together within a confined space, and equally tired looking employees sat drooped over computers that looked like they had been shipped from Doogie Howser's era. As I stood observing one such computer, it dawned on me that I hadn't been allotted a terminal yet, and so I tentatively approached Chhota Don's secretary and asked about it.

'This is the branch office,' she said in a conciliatory tone. 'You don't get a fixed terminal. Just use whatever is free.' I looked around me in confusion. Behind me, I could hear someone sniggering. I turned back. ASMs 1 and 2. I inhaled deeply and began walking towards them. ASM No. 1 immediately began punching his keyboard, and ASM No. 2 started flipping through his file.

I stopped in front of ASM No. 1. 'Hi,' I said, extending my hand. 'I'm Zoey.' ASM No. 1 merely grunted. I let my hand drop and cleared my throat. 'Chho…er…Boss said that I should speak to you about taking me to the market and introducing me to your distributors.' Without looking up, ASM No.1 growled, 'I am busy right now.' 'Er, oh, okay,' I mumbled; then nervously turned to ASM No. 2. 'Could you take me to meet your distributor today?' I asked. No response. He was staring at his file. I was wondering if I should repeat my question when he suddenly looked up, eyes half closed. 'I don't know,' he drawled cagily.

'Oh. Should I check with you after lunch then?' I prodded. He shrugged his shoulders, then continued staring at his file, fascinated, as if it held the answer to world peace. I calmed my frustration and turned away. A moment later, I was heading towards the cafeteria, my head swimming. I had thought I'd hit rock bottom in the Gurgaon guesthouse. No such luck. Turned out, there was an even deeper hole of slime waiting for me to plummet into. Just the thought of having to spend day in and day out in the company of the swearing Don and his smug ASMs was making me feel sick. *God, I wished I had died peacefully in my bed this morning.*

Later, in the cafeteria, I got myself a cup of tea to help take the edge off my panic. I was just about to sit at an empty table, when I saw someone wave at me. That someone looked familiar. That someone was...The Chester.

The Chester was a fellow Management Trainee who had been posted to the Delhi Branch, but in a different division from mine. Lara and I had bestowed that name upon him during the induction, because of his annoying habit of holding a conversation with a girl's chest instead of her face. Back in the Head Office, the two of us had avoided him like one avoids a dental appointment. But today, given that A) I was being regarded by the Delhi Branch as one regards gonorrhoea, making me feel B) uncharacteristically needy for non-hostile human contact, I was almost wildly ecstatic to see him.

I quickly walked over to join him at his table, but not without body armour of course; (body armour = cup of tea held up stiffly before upper torso). After a good thirty minutes, The Chester fished out a photo of his fiancé from his wallet and began waving it in front of my nose, while waxing rhapsodic about her many virtues. This, coupled with the fact that he had—all the while maintained contact with eyes and not chest— allowed me to, slowly and with great relief, surrender my cup to its saucer.

Feeling a tad better after my chat with a friendly face, I walked back to the office and looked around for ASM No. 2. He was nowhere to be seen. Neither were any of the other ASMs. 'Where have they gone?' I asked Chhota Don's secretary. 'To the market,' she replied. 'But I was supposed to go with them,' I almost wept. She shrugged and turned back to her computer.

'Well, that's just b***** great!' I cursed no one in particular. 'Everything is just b***** brilliant!'

Bristling, I walked to one of the empty terminals and thrust down in the chair. Then I opened a word document to type some brilliant, dazzling ideas on how to tackle my project. None came to mind. I stared instead at the blank page and brooded upon how ASM No. 2 had gone off to the market without even bothering to inform me. One hour down, I was still staring at an empty page, when Chhota Don pierced my reverie from behind. 'What the hell are you still doing here?' I jumped up a mile in the air, then twisted around to find a fierce looking Chhota Don, arms akimbo. 'I, erm, I'm working on the q-questionnaire for the p-project...' I stuttered.

He flapped. I blinked. I had been blinded by a light. What the hell was that? No, it wasn't Chhota Don's purple shirt. No, it wasn't the orange embroidery on the collar of his purple shirt either. Wait a minute...it was a tooth; a golden tooth. Chhota Don had a golden tooth and it was flashing like Bappi Lahiri.

'You should be out on the field,' he was now livid. 'How the hell are you going to map a thousand stores if you just sit here all day?!'

I attempted to speak '...I-I d-did a-ask...' then gave up. There was something about Chhota Don that made me stutter like a mindless twit.

Chhota Don stamped his foot.

'Bevkoof,' he muttered under his breath.

'Buddhu,' he added.

'Ullu,' he ended.

Then he whirled around and stomped off to his cabin. A deafening hush had enveloped the entire floor. I could feel all eyes on me. I was shaking in my seat, my face red, my eyes swimming with tears. I leaped up and rushed out towards the washroom. That man ought to have the Censor Board camped on his tongue. How dare he abuse me like that?! Captain Haddock could take verbal flagellation lessons from him. I'm not sure how long I stood in the loo, resting my forehead on the wall, wishing I could flush myself down the commode. What I do know is that when I finally did emerge from there, I was nowhere close to feeling any better.

During the next two days I continued to run around ASMs No. 1 and 2, practically begging them to introduce me to their distributors. But they kept dodging me as if I were a heap of radioactive waste. My levels of frustration were rapidly rising. The temptation to point a shot gun to their heads and demand to be taken to the market was becoming intolerable.

My only source of relief was my exchange of mails with Lara.

Dear Badri, (she wrote)

The Chennai Branch hates me. They are treating me like a social reject. *Kahaan phas gaye hum?*

Dear Srinivas, (I replied)

Ditto. I am so desperate for company that I have started hanging out with The Chester.

No! You haven't!

The Chester had now become The Shoulder. I had (quite frequently and rather sloppily) taken to crying all over it, about Chhota Don and the annoying ASMs of the fridge division.

'The ASMs don't like you because you have an MBA degree,' he explained, one day over lunch. 'They themselves have at least five years of sales experience, yet, at the end of your three-month project, you'll be handling a territory like them, with a salary higher than theirs despite having zero sales experience.'

'Unb***** likely that I'll be here at the end of three months,' I mumbled. 'B***** likely that I'll be fired by then.'

'That's what they would like to see happen,' he said. 'You have to befriend the enemy.'

'How?' I scowled. 'They hate me. What am I supposed to do? Bat my eyelashes at them? Break into a cabaret? Do an item number or two?'

The Chester grinned. 'Can you?' he drawled, 'Do an item number that is?' His eyes slowly pored over my face before resting on my chest.

I frowned, becoming aware of a sudden and overwhelming urge to hit him. Exit left stage: The Shoulder. Enter right stage: The Chester.

Luckily for him, his eyes veered back to my face before I could organize my fist. I darted him a dirty look instead (of the Class A variety), then found myself rewinding to the last thought and brooding over it. How on earth was I supposed to be-friend the enemy?

'You know,' The Chester broke into my thoughts, 'If the ASMs are not taking you to the market, you should go yourself. Why depend on them?' I looked at him keenly, then decided that he had a point. After which, I walked back into the office, switched off my computer, picked up my bag and proceeded to walk out.

'Where are you going?' ASM No. 1 asked. *Oh. So now he was talking to me, was he?* He was leaning against his terminal, arms crossed, eyes watchful.

I pretended to throw my hair over my shoulder, and gave him a haughty look. 'To the market,' I said airily. Then I flounced past him with my nose so high in the air, that I'm surprised I didn't smack my chin against the ceiling on the way out.

Downstairs, I quickly flagged an auto and ushered my tentative self into it. Five minutes into the ride, I noticed that the auto dude kept squinting at me shiftily through the rear view mirror. Fifteen minutes into the ride, I noticed that the auto was going around Delhi in circles. Twenty minutes into the ride:

- Number of shifty looks from auto dude: Zillion.
- Number of circles made around Delhi: Zillion.
- Destination Khan Market: Still Elusive.

My imagination was now beginning to run riot. In the absence of any other emotion, my default setting was terror. I caught the Auto Man's eye in the mirror. '*Kahaan ja rahe ho?*' I yelled shrilly. '*Kabse gol gol ghoom rahe ho!*' Auto Man didn't reply. My blood began to bubble. '*Bas yahaan ruko. Mujhe abhi utarna hai!* Auto Man rode on, feigning deafness. Panic rising, I screamed into his ear: '*Main Karate Black Belt hoon!!!*' This was a fat lie, of course, but I was so traumatized. Still no reply. The auto rumbled on. I was just about to fling myself out of it, when, suddenly, Khan Market appeared in front of me. I fell back, almost ecstatic with relief.

As I was preparing to alight, I caught the Auto Man giving me one of those 'the-idiots-that-I-have-to-put-up-with' looks in the rear view mirror. I scowled at him, snatched up my bag and scrambled out. But then Auto Man told me the fare, and my heart once again flirted with a cardiac arrest. A long argument followed, steam whooshing out of my ears as I wrangled with him over the amount; all the while missing the Mumbai autos with a sense of sick desperation. Finally, aware of the fact that despite my bargaining efforts, I was still being robbed in broad daylight, I thrust the money into his hand, stung him a death glare and stormed off utterly frustrated.

I came to a halt outside the first consumer durable outlet to my right. Jangling with nerves, I pulled out a questionnaire from my bag and walked into the store. The owner sat behind a counter while his assistants hovered around their scant two customers like vultures. As soon as I walked in, an assistant obsequiously turned his head to me and broke into a big smile. 'Namaste,' he said, quickly walking over. 'Namaste,' I replied, nodding. 'Ji, aapki kya help kar sakta hoon?' he asked, looking expectant. 'Er, actually mujhe…' I looked down at my questionnaire and suddenly felt sheepish; I glanced at the two customers in the store and felt a stab of envy. Suddenly I too wanted to be a customer. I too wanted to be King.

Without warning, I heard my mouth say, 'iPods rakhte ho?' The assistant smiled wider. 'Ji haan. Bilkul. Hum iPods rakhte hain…Aaiye please,' Then he bowed. I half expected him to roll out a red carpet. Delighted, I wanted to pat him on his head, but instead, simply beamed. 'Zara madam ke liye paani laana,' he demanded of another assistant. I beamed wider. Soon enough, I was out of the store, my bag a little heavier than when I'd entered it, my eyes guiltily flitting around in fear of witnesses. 'Coward,' I heard a voice in my head scold as I started pulling out the new acquisition in my bag with covert interest. I wavered. Damn. Not only had I not filled my questionnaire, I was now broke.

I had taken a few steps outside the shop when I heard a loud, squelchy sound. I looked down and froze. My adorable, shiny new Aldo, the only piece of extravagance in my entire wardrobe—three inches deep in gooey dung. In slow motion, I looked down and stared agape at it. What in heavens name was going on? I wondered befuddled. Why in Hades was I standing here in some random market in Delhi with my foot wrapped in dung when I could have been at home in Pune listening to my mom rave about meeting some nice boy?

Very soon, I was vigorously scraping the heel of my shoe against the pavement. 'I HATE MY LIFE,' I yelled, heedless of the curious glances of passers-by. Just then my phone buzzed through my bag. One foot in the air, I began rummaging for it. Where the hell was my phone? Damn. I hated my hold-all bag—I could NEVER find a THING in it. NEVER. Ah. Found it. A text from Lara: Deep in Shit!!! Only mapped twenty outlets so far!

I smirked. Deep in Shit, was she? Hah! She didn't know the half of it.

Soon, I was once again spanning the chasm between wishy and washy as I lingered outside another durable store. Should I go in? Should I not? Should I go? Should I not? Finally, I squared my shoulders and with questionnaire in hand, nervously lumbered into the store. This time I ignored the shop assistants and resolutely paced directly towards the storeowner.

'Ji?' he said, ruefully taking in the trail of dung marks I had left behind on his floor.

'Erm, main survey kar rahi hoon,' I mumbled pinkly, waving my questionnaire at him.

He blinked, unimpressed, still pointedly scrutinizing the dung marks.

I smiled bashfully, feeling utterly lame. 'Mujhe aapse kuch sawaal poonchne the...'

He didn't show his aggravation, but I sensed it was close.

'Aap fridge ke kaun kaunse brands rakhte ho?' I whispered.

This time, there was a scowl. A very elaborate one too. Then he folded his arms and pursed his lips in an unmistakable *Excuse me behenji. Do you mind?* look. I turned pinker and showed him another sheepish smile. He narrowed his eyes, then jerked his head to one of his shop assistants and snapped his finger at him.

I twirled around in alarm, half expecting his assistant to come charging at me to throw me out of the store. Instead, the assistant picked up a mop from behind the counter and grumpily began mopping the dung marks off the floor.

I looked at the storeowner apologetically, face now a bright red.

He gave me a stony look, then snapped, 'Sab brands.'

'Eh?' I frowned.

'Hum sab brands rakhte hain,' he growled.

'Er, sab brands? Kaunse brands?' I prodded daftly.

He took a deep breath, then seemed to grit his teeth. 'Dekhiye memsaab, humaare paas time nahi hai. Hum bahut busy hain.'

I felt sick. Desperate, I clasped my hands and begged, 'Please uncle...Please...'

He gave me a long contemplative look, then decided to take pity on me. A short while later, I walked out of the store, my first filled questionnaire in hand. Alright then, I cackled, clapping my hands in glee. One outlet down. Hurrah! The only issue was that I still had 999 outlets to go. That bit felt less wonderful.

Back home, I had a lonely pint with Coolio, my second hand J&K (Direct Cool) fridge (which, I had managed to get for a steal and which was the only piece of furniture in my flat apart from a rickety bed.) After The Chester, Coolio was my next new best friend in town. Never mind the fact that the insides of Coolio were like those of a Somalian victim: empty, except for a week-old, half-eaten apple.

My days slipped into an uneasy routine. Mornings involved dodging Chhota Don, chasing ASMs in circles and between the two, blowing around aimlessly like a wisp of tumbleweed. Afternoons involved haggling with seedy auto rickshaw men and bombarding unsuspecting durable storeowners with a whole bunch of inane questions. Two weeks gone, and while I had managed to map more than a dozen outlets, I still hadn't met any of the distributors.

It was a Friday afternoon, when Chhota Don called out from his cabin to come in with my first progress report. I collected the report and entered his room, feeling as if my stomach was spilling out.

'Have you met all the distributors?' Chhota Don asked, as soon as I stepped in…

'N-no-sir,' I stuttered.

He frowned. 'Which ones have you met?'

'N-none sir,' I stuttered again, 'b-but I've mapped…'

Chhota Don's beard twitched. 'You haven't met any of the distributors yet? What the DEVIL have you been doing all this time then?!'

I blinked daftly at him for a few seconds, then mumbled, 'S-sir, I have been going to the market on my own…'

'None of the bigger stores are going to give you the correct information,' he admonished, 'unless you are introduced to them by the ASMs or the distributor salesman.'

'Erm, um…'

'Why haven't you met the distributors yet?' he demanded.

What was I supposed to tell him? That I had been chasing ASMs 1 and 2 in circles for an introduction only to discover that they would rather stick a fork in their eye than take me to the market? I couldn't. Not at the risk of coming off as a pathetic snitch. So, instead, I studied my toenails, which suddenly seemed utterly enthralling. A few seconds later, when I mustered the courage to look up at Chhota Don, I noticed that his jaw looked a little clenched and the blood vessel on his forehead looked ready to split. 'Dhingra!!!' he bayed. 'Get in here!!!'

ASM No. 1 rushed in, all meek and willing, like Mogambo's sidekick. 'Haanji sir…Boliye sir…' I looked at him with revulsion. I was pretty sure that if Chhota Don so wished, ASM No. 1 would get down on all fours right then and wipe his bottom for him.

'Why the hell haven't you introduced her yet to Mr Singh?' Chhota Don roared. His golden tooth was flashing brighter than usual. I wondered if he'd had it polished. 'She has to map the entire city! The project is a waste of time but The CEO is personally looking into it. You'd better introduce her today.' ASM No. 1 nodded vigorously. His forehead had broken into a sweat. Hah! Served him right. I peeked at Chhota Don, feeling a sudden stab of affection for him. It was all I could do to stop myself from walking over to him and patting his head in approval.

Soon, I found myself trotting out of the office behind a disgruntled ASM No.1, who was making his frustration known through several huffs, puffs, and twists of mouth. Once out of the building, he stopped in front of his scooter and pulled out his helmet. I took in his two-wheeler uneasily. *Was I supposed to travel with him on that?* I had not had much experience riding pillion on a scooter. Should I straddle it, I wondered. Or sit facing one side? I checked back on ASM No.1. He was throwing invisible hate bombs in my direction. I bristled. *I too would rather go bald than sit on the back of your damn scooter*, I wanted to howl at him.

'Chalein Madam?' he said, voice dripping with sarcasm. I resisted the urge to wallop his head with his helmet; instead walked towards the scooter and gingerly sat on it sideways. Then I clenched the handle on my side and prayed that I don't fall off mid-way. Something told me that if I did, ASM No. 1 would not bother to stop.

Twenty minutes later, our scooter pulled over in front of the office of Mr Singh, the South Delhi distributor.

'Head Office se aayi hain,' ASM No. 1 told him without preamble, as the two of us walked in. Mr Singh had been picking his nose unreservedly. On seeing us, he slowly abandoned his nasal excavation to run his eyes up and down my form.

Feeling like a commodity on display, I crossed my arms and tried to quell my outrage. Realizing that ASM No. 1 wasn't going to say anything further, I cleared my throat and proceeded to tell Mr Singh what my project involved. Shady Singh smirked, then cast a conspiratorial look at ASM No. 1, who immediately frowned sullenly in response. Leaning back in his chair, Shady Singh once again turned to ogle me. Suddenly, he let out a loud belch, like the smack of thunder.

I started, and gripped at my heart with fright. What *was* with all the belching? Was it some sort of a pastime peculiar to the capital city? The aversion in my head must have escaped to my face because Shady Singh's eyes narrowed. His attention still pinned unashamedly on my face, he called out to his salesman.

A middle-aged man with paan-stained teeth and long side burns walked to the front of the office from across the street, wheeling along his rickety scooter. Shady Singh turned to him, his nose twitching. 'Oh ji, madam ko market le jaiyyo zara, apne scooter-shooter pe.' Scooter-man glanced at me, then at Shady Singh, 'Aaj market bandh hai,' he grunted.

'Accha koi nahin…Monday ko dikhaiyyo.' Then he pelted me with one last shady look, before waving a dismissive hand at me and resuming his nasal excavation.

That evening, desperate to get out of my head and seized by a burst of recklessness, I accompanied The Chester to a nearby pub. My system had been protesting all week due to the prolonged spell of alcohol-deprivation. The situation, I decided, warranted split-second remedying, particularly in the wake of recent events. Beer glut was the need of the hour.

After a while, I had lost count of how much beer I had downed. All I knew was that I had begun to slur, and that instead of one Chester, I could now see two of them swimming before me. I rubbed my eyes and peered at each one in turn.

'Do you have a boyfriend?' I heard his voice, as if through a cloud.

I rubbed my eyes again, then shook my head hard. Two Chesters had now morphed into three. I let out a drunken giggle.

'No,' I mumbled, taking another swig. God, it was hot in here. I clunked my pint down on the table, picked up the menu and began flapping it feverishly.

The Chester was now smiling toothily at me. 'I'm not getting married till December,' he said; he paused to take a swill of his beer, then chuckled, 'So technically, I'm still available.' He chuckled again.

I blinked. I didn't like his phony chuckle. *And, wait, was that a lecherous look he was giving me?* I jiggled my head. *No. Can't be. I was being paranoid.* I took another large glug and belched.

'So are you interested?' he asked, a moment later.

I wrinkled my nose. 'Interesshted in wha…[hic]'

Pause. Another lecherous look? Hic. Definitely Not. Can't be.

'In a fling…'

I froze, mid-hiccup.

I'm not sure how long I sat there, open-mouthed, eyes blinking, but luckily my Fury eventually made an entrance. 'Let me handle this bugger,' Fury growled, folding up its sleeves. And just like that I unfroze, whacked my bottle on the table, narrowed my eyes to slits and told The Chester that the only kind of fling I was interested in was the kind that involved my fist making contact with his jaw.

Half an hour later, I tottered into my flat and banged the door shut. Then, I kicked off my shoes and staggered into the kitchen. Aaaah Coolio! Hic. *Coolio!* I lunged forward, flung my arms around it and began to howl like a baby. 'Coolio,' I blubbed, sniffing loudly, 'you are now my authorishhed Bessht Friend No. 1.'

5

Guide to cocktail making. Cocktail: 'Bloody Delhi'

Ingredients:
- *1 Me (Floundering Management Trainee. 5 feet 9 inches of cluelessness)*
- *1 Chhota Don (Delhi Sales Head. 5 feet 2 inches of gaalis.)*
- *2 ASMs (Area Sales Managers. Sell fridges. Wish they could stick me in one. Because I am clueless, yet I am paid more.)*
- *1 Shady Singh (South Delhi Distributor. Shrewd Businessman. Shady Man.)*
- *1 Scooter-man (Shady Singh's Salesman. Special power: Rides scooter.)*
- *And finally, a gazillion consumer durable outlets (Give or take a few.)*

Take a cocktail glass and throw 'me' in to the deep end. Then, add ASMs 1 and 2. Stir furiously, so that I have to chase them in circles even to get directions to the loo. Now, add 1 Shady Singh. Ensure that he is operating at 100% leching capacity. Then wait for him to emit a loud burp, before directing his lecherous eyes back at me. Next, add the gazillion durable outlets. Dunk them in so deep, that I struggle to reach them in

those notorious Delhi autos. Just as I am drowning, throw in
a lifesaver. (Is it a bird? Is it a plane? No. It's Scooter-man.
On a rickety scooter. Reaching for the gazillion outlets. With
me on the back seat!)

Things were looking up. In the last two weeks, Scooter-man
had been flying me all over South Delhi on his rickety scooter
and thanks to him, my durable store count was now well over a
hundred. But it wasn't just Scooter-man who had made my life
take a turn for the better. There was another reason why things
had suddenly begun to feel *copeable* again.

So, this is what happened. Two weeks ago, on the Saturday
following the Chester Incident, having spent the entire morning
flailing about in a pool filled with one-third part anger and two-
thirds part self pity, I decided to drag myself to the nearest book
store. After about twenty-five minutes (spent sifting through
chick-lits with happy endings and feeling even more miserable),
I found myself circling around the 'Self Help' section of the
store. Now, I hadn't been to this section of a bookstore in a
while, not since I had picked up 'How to Become a Corporate
Shark' back in my B-School days. A whole lot of good that book
did for me, because one and a half years later, I felt nothing like
a corporate shark and everything like a confused ostrich.
Personally, I have always hated self-help books. They are nothing
but a load of condescending gunk.

Shortly, however, I found myself standing right in the middle
of that section; surreptitiously leafing through a copy of (the
unbelievable) 'Six Habits of Highly Successful People'. 'Good
choice,' said one of the bookstore helpers, bobbing up from
nowhere. I slapped the book shut and threw him an impatient

glance. 'We sold ten copies of this book in the last two hours,' he said.

'I don't plan to buy it. I was just leafing through it,' I averred. The bookstore helper shrugged.

'I mean, for God's sake, look at me…' I burst out.

The bookstore helper looked.

'…Do I look like I need a self-help book?'

The bookstore helper looked harder.

'…Because, of course, I don't need a self-help book!'

The bookstore helper looked doubtful.

'Self-help books are just a heap of sanctimonious rubbish!'

The bookstore helper smiled, then gave me a sly, all-knowing wink, as if he was privy to a moment in my near future that I had no clue was coming. Ignoring him, I trundled around to the corner, with the book, all set to march to the storeowner and report about how he was peddling a load of hogwash.

And hence, it came as a big surprise when, in a bit, I found myself (guiltily) scurrying out of the book store with a copy of…you guessed it…'Six Habits of Highly Successful People' tucked away in my bag. The *bigger* surprise: That I stayed up till 4 a.m. the next morning reading that book as if it were the latest Harry Potter. The *biggest* surprise: That, in the weeks that followed, I found myself slowly notching my way up to the altar of Career Zen!

The Six Habits of Highly Successful People:

1. <u>Believe in yourself</u>. Tick. Woke up one morning (two days after reading the book), looked in the mirror, tossed my hair over my shoulder and said out loud: I am Zoey Verma. I am Super Woman on Super Important Mission.

Self raised an eyebrow. 'Yeah, right,' it scorned.

I was not deterred. Recorded my voice on a tape (as per instructions in the book) and played it every night for a week before going to sleep.

Woke up in the morning (two weeks later), looked in the mirror, tossed my hair over my shoulder and said out aloud: I am Zoey Verma. I am Super Woman on Super Important mission.

Self gave me a high five. 'You go girlfriend,' it sang.

(Hoping that Self does not snap out of hypnosis anytime soon.)

2. Remember your goal. Tick. Have committed Wimp-eater's words, 'Map every outlet, else *will eat you alive*,' to memory. Can now recite them during all five stages of sleep.

The other day, had to pull Self to office (after a tiring day in market), to work on dreaded status report. Was so tired, ended up flopping over keyboard and snoring instead (luckily keyboard was in far corner of hall, safely out of Chhota Don's line of vision). Had to be nudged out of REM cycle by one of the pouty girls from the servicing team. 'Are you okay?' she asked.

Me: 'Er, yes.'
She: 'Who is Peter?'
Me: 'Peter who?'
She: 'Peter the pimp.'
Me: 'Peter the what?'
She: 'Why are you hanging around with pimps?'
Me: 'Eh?'
She: 'You were talking in your sleep.'
Me: 'Oh?'
She: 'Some pimp called Peter wants to eat you alive.'
Me: 'Ahhh...!'

3. <u>Be committed</u>. Tick. Am so committed that have developed durable-outlet radar. Can now spot a durable outlet all the way out in China. One Saturday, went to Lajpat Nagar market to do some shoe shopping. Time taken to spot shoe store in market: Forty minutes. Time taken to spot all thirteen durable stores in market: Forty seconds!

Post-it to Self: Submit application for Guinness Book of World Records.

4. <u>Be focussed</u>. Am so focussed that, these days, when I go to a market I am like Arnold Schwarzenegger in Terminator 1. I target a store, I barge into it, I shoot questions at the owner and then, I coolly breeze out. The other day, in Green Park market, I'd just slid out of my tenth store, when I spotted yet another durable store to my left. *I must have missed this one*, I thought and marched towards it. Once inside, I rounded on the retailer and opened my mouth wide: 'Ji, aap kya-kya rakhte ho? Kaun-kaun se brands rakhte ho? Kitne units rakhte ho? Kitne—'

'Madam, madam, madam,' the retailer chirped in, 'aap is outlet mein already aa chooki hain. Humne already aapko sab jawaab de diye hain…'

Jesus, I thought out aloud, I have come a full circle. I must have covered the entire market. This means I can stop for now. I gave the retailer a big grin and patted my back in delight.

5. <u>Be thorough</u>. Tick. Am so thorough that, the other day, on my way to some random relative's wedding, when my durable outlet radar started beeping hysterically, I couldn't help flapping my arms wildly and clamouring ear-shatteringly 'Ruko!!' in the auto driver's ear. Auto driver screeched auto to a halt and looked at me in the rear view mirror like I was a fruitcake on the loose. But I didn't care. 'Ek minute, ruko,' I panted and tumbled

out of the auto. Then I dashed to the durable outlet and rattled off my questions. Two minutes later, I was back in the auto, happily waving the filled questionnaire at the auto driver. Auto driver was still looking at me like I was a fruitcake on the loose. But, hah. What did he know? He was not High-Flying Super Woman on Super Important Mission.

6. <u>Be thick-skinned</u>. Tick. Post repeated instructions to my thin skin to sprout rhino-like layer, I was now deflecting *gaalis* flying at me from Chhota Don like a Jedi warrior. The other day, barely had I entered the office, when Chhota Don marched towards me, his Anger preceding him.

'Good morning Boss!' I sang, flashing him a big, blinding grin. Chhota Don blinked, momentarily faltering. 'Hmmph,' he grunted, quickly recovering; then he puffed up his chest and began to yell, 'Where the hell...'

'Beautiful morning, isn't it?' I chirped, deliberately interrupting him—a feat I would not have accomplished had it not been for the recent possession of my body by Rhett Butler's ghost. I now, frankly, couldn't give a damn. I had developed a thick skin and I was immune to Chhota Don and his gaalis.

Chhota Don's face furrowed into a scowl. His Anger was fast acquiring a companion: Peeve. He narrowed his eyes and resumed shouting, 'Where the hell is your progress report?! The Head Office wants an update by end of day! How many outlets have you mapped...I want a...'

'Have nearly finished mapping the South zone, Boss,' I said, flashing him another dazzling grin. 'You will have the report in your inbox within an hour, Boss.'

Anger and Peeve looked at each other, utterly bewildered, the wind sucked out of both. A second later, Peeve turned to Anger. 'I think it's time to go.' Anger nodded in acceptance.

Shoulders bent, they humbly slunk away. 'Hmm...ok then,' Chhota Don said petulantly, feeling betrayed by his companions, then turned around sulkily and flopped back to his cabin.

At 12.30 p.m., the report was mailed to Chhota Don. At 12.31 p.m. I got up to leave for the market. 'The report?' demanded Chhota Don, through the glass door of his cabin. Everyone turned to look at me. 'In your inbox,' I said and waved a happy wave. Everyone looked visibly impressed. At 12.32 p.m., I was out the door.

Yep, things were definitely looking up.

And so, a few days later, when my mom called to tell me that 'Nice Boy from Mumbai' was in Delhi for a short visit and that I should meet him, I (because things were looking up and I was bursting with good will), found myself smiling into the phone and singing, 'Okay, why not?'

Of course, a week later, my insides were singing a slightly different tune.

It was a Saturday morning, almost noon actually. I had just tumbled out of bed and was rummaging through Coolio for food that could make do brunch (there was none; unless a bottle of acetone and a peel of banana qualified), when I got a text from Nice Boy. UR MM GVE ME UR NO. WNT 2 CTCH UP 4 CFY?

Bugger. Nice Boy! I had almost forgotten. I squinted at the message. What the hell was CFY? I rubbed my eyes and peered at the message again. Could someone get some vowels please? And while you're at it, some consonants too? And why was Nice Boy texting? Didn't he have the guts to call? I leaned against Coolio and massaged my temple. *God. Why had I agreed to meet him? What had I been thinking?* For a moment I thought of texting him that I was in the throes of an epileptic fit, which was likely to last for a month at least, but then decided that between meeting Nice Boy and my mom's melodrama, the former was a more digestible option.

And so, soon enough, despite the missing vowels, consonants and guts, I wrote to Nice Boy that I would meet him at a nearby 'CFY' shop. I had a plan of course. The plan was to assign not more than thirty minutes of my life to Nice Boy. I had a feeling that anything more than that would be a recipe for suicide.

At the appointed time, I reached said 'CFY' shop. Nice Boy hadn't shown up yet. I settled into a chair in a corner and whipped out my paperback. Twelve minutes down—still no sign of him. I checked my phone hoping for a message cancelling the meeting. No such luck. Another few minutes went by. I was just contemplating getting up and leaving when in walked a thin, nervous looking specimen with oily hair cleanly parted on the side and thick glasses neatly perched on his nose. Now, I hadn't seen Nice Boy's photo but something told me this was Nice Boy. He had 'Stable Boy' who 'Liked Family Values' written all over him.

Nice Boy approached my table tentatively. 'You are Zoey, right?' he whispered. I nodded. 'I'm Sunny,' he said in a thin, girly voice. Aha. No wonder he hadn't called. That effeminate voice wasn't exactly a ticket to Great First Impressions.

'Hi,' I said unenthusiastically, sizing him up. Yellow-striped shirt, yellow-strapped watch and yellow-stained teeth. Yep, he sure as hell was sunny.

The waiter arrived. We ordered a cappuccino and a Lemon Iced tea, then lapsed into an awkward silence. I studied the menu. He studied his thumbs. When our orders eventually arrived, he took the huge cup of cappuccino in his hands and peered at me from behind it. I looked at my watch. God, another eighteen minutes to go. I inhaled deeply. When I looked up again, he was still peering at me.

'Something on my nose?' I let fly.

He smiled sheepishly and turned red. 'You don't look like your profile pic,' he finally said.

What the hell did that mean? Did I look uglier in person? More wrinkled? WHAT? Elaborate, you dolt.

'Different, how?' I asked.

'Just different,' he replied evasively. I crossed my arms defiantly, pride forbidding me to probe further.

'So what are your hobbies?' he asked. Hah. Mr Beacon of originality.

'I like to read,' I said dully.

'Ooh,' he brightened. 'I like reading too'

Well, well, what do you know…the man read. I sat up in my chair. Nice Boy's cool quotient had just risen a notch from zilch.

'What do you read?' I asked him, my tone much milder.

'Non fiction stuff,' he was quick to reply.

'Oh, you mean, like biographies?' I asked, with interest.

'No, I mean, like, books on insurance, you know, like, general insurance, life insurance, health insurance, corporate insurance…you see, I work in insurance.'

'Right,' I offered. Cool *quotient sliding back to zilch. Repeat, cool quotient sliding back to zilch.*

'I am now reading *Insurance for Dummies*,' he announced. 'It's an interesting book. Very informative. Have you read it?'

'Er, no.' *Cool quotient turning negative. Repeat, cool quotient turning negative.*

A long awkward pause followed. I finally broke it with 'So

what are you looking for in a girl?' LAME, I know…but someone had to say something.

'Well,' he started, 'she should be nice…'

Big surprise.

'She should be homely…'

Yawn.

'She should have good family values…'

Ahem.

'She should know how to cook…'

Barf.

'She should have a job…'

Hmmph.

'She should…'

My patience was beginning to run thin. It was time to give a reality check to Mr I-Want-A-Super-Woman-Because-I've-Never-Looked-At-Myself-In-A-Mirror.

'Guess what,' I said, cutting him short, 'I do NOT know how to cook.'

Nice Boy blinked from behind his cup.

'And, it's likely that I might be JOBLESS three months from now…And let me tell you, I am definitely not HOME…'

'Why?' he cut in, mouth agape.

'Why what?' I retorted, raising a defiant brow. 'Can't cook, you mean?'

'Yes, I mean, no, I mean, that too but—but-but why will you be jobless?'

I choked. 'Because my boss thinks I'm a joker.'

He looked nonplussed for a second, sounded a weak 'Oh', but then he recovered. And how! 'That's okay,' he declared brightly. 'I think my income can support both of us…at least for the first year of marriage…I'm sure you will get another job eventually…and then you might want to reflect on taking care of your savings…look at some investment options, you know…I could help you with that…do you have an insurance policy?'

'Eh?' I sputtered, floored…

He took that as a cue to launch into a seven-minute monologue about the history of insurance, during which time I had lapsed into a coma. When I re-surfaced, he was still carrying on about the difference between a Gold and a Platinum Insurance policy. Clearly, it was time for me to cut him short and stage my exit.

'Eeesh!' I faked suddenly, looking at my watch. Nice Boy flinched, blinked a couple of times. 'Have to be somewhere,' I bounded up and sang, 'sorry, late already, must run!'

Nice Boy looked flustered. 'Er…but when can we meet again? I am in Delhi again, end of next month…'

Jeez. Was he really as thick as he looked? 'How about the 31st of next month, then?' I asked, picking up my bag.

He nodded. Once, twice. Three times. Then, half-way through his fourth nod, he stopped directly. 'But-but September has only 30 days,' he bleated.

Right on, Sherlock.

'You don't say,' I said with a wink. Then I twirled on my Aldos and waltzed out.

Really. It was time to sit my mom down and enlighten her on The Weirdoes That Inhabit The Online Matrimonial World.

I was in an auto, halfway home, when Lara texted:

So, how was Nice Boy? (wink-wink)

You mean Dullsville on two legs? I texted back.

Hehehehe. Gag

Not funny. Don't laugh.

Ok. Ok. Will not laugh. Hehehehe. Gag.
Oh shut up.

Later that afternoon, at home, I found myself brooding on the subject of my Ex (the one with whom I'd had a nasty break-up, but we'll get to that part later). Now, I hadn't thought of him in over two months; but today after that disastrous experience with Nice Boy, I hadn't been able to stop thinking about him. I blamed Nice Boy. He made The Ex look like George Clooney and sound like Amitabh Bachchan (quite a feat, given that The Ex is no stud); and suddenly I was feeling all low and lonely and in desperate need of an Ex Fix.

I will not call or message The Ex, I firmly told myself. I would much rather drown in a tub of watermelon ice cream, I decided, marching determinedly towards Coolio. Tequila shots would have been even better, but since I was still nursing a grudge—the size of Australia—against The Chester, and hence couldn't go pubbing with him, a tub of watermelon ice cream would have to do.

A couple of hours later, I lay snuggled up in bed, empty tub in hand, watching *One Fine Day* for the millionth time. My phone buzzed. Thinking it to be a text from my mom wanting a lowdown on Nice Boy, I ignored it. A few minutes more and my phone buzzed again. I bristled. Couldn't she take a hint? Then I shook my head. Of course, she couldn't. My mom was thick-skinned with a capital T. For all I knew, she had secretly co-authored 'Six Habits of Highly Successful People'.

I grabbed my phone impatiently and clicked on the first message. It wasn't from mom. It was from Vodafone. *Hello! Your mobile phone bill is due. Please pay to avoid uninterrupted services. For bill details SMS BILL to 111 (toll free).* I railed out a series of cuss words, then glanced at the second message.

My heart skipped a beat. Hi. How've you been? Been thinking about you. It was my Ex…

★

So?! Did u reply to him?!
From: Lara (Work)
Received @ 12.03 a.m.

Hope you didn't…I mean, do you really want to go down that road again?
From: Lara (Work)
Received @ 12.08 a.m.

Pls tell me u didn't! Anyway why aren't you picking up my calls?
From: Lara (Work)
Received @ 12.13 a.m.

Zoey Verma! Have you slept off already?!!
From: Lara (Mob)
Received @ 12.22 a.m.

6

The following Monday morning I stood outside Shady Singh's store, waiting for Scooter-man to take me to the market. I was not in the best of moods. Just a while ago, I'd had Infuriating Conversation No. 999 with my mom. It had started innocuously enough (as had Infuriating Conversations No. 1 to 998 in the past); but by the end of it, as usual, I had wanted to pull my hair apart.

Infuriating Conversation No. 999 with mom

Mom (cheerily): 'Did you receive the laddoos that I couriered?'

Me (preoccupied): 'Yes. I did.'

Mom (probing): 'Did you eat the laddoos?'

Me (vaguely): 'Yes. I did.'

Mom (persistent): 'Did you like the laddoos?'

Me (patiently): 'Yes. I did.'

Me (suddenly remembering to ask): 'Should I store the laddoos in the fridge?'

Mom (can't believe she has been asked such a daft question): 'Hain? Which idiot keeps laddoos in the fridge?'

Mom again (full-tilt): 'Did you meet that nice boy?'

Me (dazed by mom's sudden skip from laddoos to Nice Boy)

Mom (impatiently): 'Well, have you met him?'

Me (reluctantly): 'Yeah. I have.'

Mom (happily): 'Isn't he nice?'

Me (caught on back foot): 'Erm...'

Mom (merrily): 'Isn't he stable?'

Me (still on back foot): 'Aaa...'

Mom (singing): 'So when are you meeting him again?'

Me (finally recovering): 'I refuse to meet him again.'

Mom (screeching): 'Wha...? What?! What do you mean???'

Me (holding the phone a mile off from my ear)

Mom (still screeching): 'Hain? Why don't you want to meet him???'

Me (long-sufferingly): 'Because I didn't like him.'

Mom (yelling): 'But why didn't you like him?'

Me (irritably): 'Because we are not on the same wavelength.'

Mom (roughly): 'Why? What wavelength are you on?'

Me (retorting): 'Don't know. But it's not the one that he is on.'

Mom (unimpressed): 'Pah! All this wavelength-shavelength ...it is all nonsense. He is a very nice boy. You are being very choosy.'

Me (pressing my forehead): 'I have to go mom, I'm busy.'

Mom (pissed off): 'What busy? You are always busy. Don't give me this busy-shizy. Don't give me th...'

Me (cutting in): 'Have to go mom. Will call you soon. Bye.'

Mom (even more pissed off): 'But-but...'

Exactly five seconds later, my phone beeped. I flicked a burning look at it. A *text* from my mom this time.

There is another nice boy who has expressed interest in your profile. I have given him your phone number.

I closed my eyes and bit my lip. I felt so angry I wanted to hurl a shoe at someone. A teeny part of my brain, however, the part that wasn't roaring in rage, whispered to me in a voice filled with awe: *You've got to hand it to that woman! The sheer tenacity! She is like a pit bull with blinkers on!*

Two minutes later, a scooter drew up outside the store. Ah. Scooter-man! Finally. I squinted at my watch. He was rather late. But it wasn't Scooter-man, I realized, as the man dismounted and pulled off his helmet. It was ASM No.1. As soon as he spotted me, his face broke into a frown. He flung me a dirty look, then tromped clean past me into the store. I glared at his receding form. Just as I was contemplating hurling a shoe at it, a car pulled up right in front of me, and a bald, heavy-set man scrambled out. Damn, I cursed. Shady Singh. Could the morning get any worse?

In the last two weeks, I had successfully managed to avoid Shady Singh by insisting on meeting Scooter-man well before Shady Singh's usual arrival time. But now Scooter-man was twenty minutes late and Shady Singh was ten minutes early and consequently I was forced to look around wildly for routes of escape. Argh. Bugger. Too late. Shady Singh had spotted me. 'Namaste,' he hailed out. 'Namaste,' I nodded. 'Gupta*ji* abhi tak nahi aayein?' he asked, stroking his bald pate. 'Nahin' I said, shaking my head. 'Toh andar aaiyein na please,' he said, smiling lewdly. I reluctantly followed him into the store. Damn Scooter-man. *Where the hell was he?*

ASM no. 1 was already seated inside, puffing on a cigarette in a corner, looking very much at home. Shady Singh greeted him noisily before scuffling behind his counter. I pulled up a stool and sat next to ASM No. 1, my eyes all the while darting to the street, hoping to see Scooter-man riding in. Some minutes and a round of nauseatingly sweet tea later, there was still no sign of Scooter-man. Meanwhile, ASM No. 1 had been filling in Shady Singh with the news that, as part of a scheme for high-performing distributors, J&K planned to send him abroad for an all-expenses-paid vacation. Shady Singh perked up, his bald head flushed and shining. 'Kahaan bhejne wale hain mujhe?' he asked.

'Malaysia,' ASM No. 1 replied.

Shady Singh didn't look too thrilled. Shrugging his plump shoulders, he said, 'Arre, Malaysia kyon bhej rahe ho? Bangkok bhejo…kam se kam…wahaan gori chamdi toh milegi…'

ASM No. 1 chortled. *God. Where the hell was I? On the sets of some B-grade Bollywood movie?*

'Hum kya karein Sir ji…' ASM No. 1 shrugged, throwing me a sly look, 'Head Office waalon ne Malaysia decide kar liya.'

Taking the cue, Shady Singh turned to face me. Spreading his plump, ringed hands on the counter, he said, 'Madam, aap Head Office se aayi hain. Zara unko bolo humko Bangkok bhejein.' ASM No. 1 chortled again. Could I clobber his head with a fridge from where I was sitting? Alas, no.

Mercifully, Scooter-man chose that precise moment to slip into sight. Yay! Finally, I could get the hell out of here! Unfortunately, I vaulted off the stool with such speed that I lost my balance and went flying. Before I knew it, I lay startled over the counter, chin smacked on its glass top, Shady Singh's paunch practically in my face. I stared at it, dumb with horror and mortification, then blinked. I could see stars. My chin was hurting so much it was a wonder it hadn't broken open. Somehow, I managed to unglue myself from the counter, pick up my bag and without looking left or right, run towards Scooter-man. I wasn't sure if the sound I heard on my way out was that of ASM No.1 and Shady Singh convulsing with laughter, but I didn't look back to find out.

That evening, back in office as I filed my status report (while nursing a bandaged chin), my Outlook announced the arrival of a mail from The Beaver. Curious, I clicked on it right away. *Dear Zoey*, The Beaver wrote, *Due to some budget cuts in the Kolkata Branch I am being transferred to the Delhi office.* He then went on to ramble for another two thousand words about other irrelevant stuff, which I never got around to reading, because my eyes remained fixed on those first few words. The Beaver was coming to Delhi? Hurrah! Hallelujah! I hugged myself and grinned from ear to ear. I was just about to break into a delirious dance, when a thought blew into my head: *Zoey Verma, are you seriously feeling exhilarated at the prospect of The Beaver? That annoying little shiny faced, over enthusiastic thing?! Woman, you have got to get yourself a life!* Lara seemed to echo that sentiment because later that night, when I texted her the news of The Beaver's arrival along with four exclamation marks and three smiley emoticons, her reply was:

Excuse me, but who the hell are you? And what the hell have you done to Zoey Verma?

The Beaver arrived at the Delhi office exactly a week later. I ran across the floor to greet him as if I were meeting a long lost friend after a decade of war. He looked thrown for a few seconds, then managed to recover, smiling weakly. 'What happened to your chin?' he asked, peering curiously at it. My hand flew to the bruise. 'Ah, nothing,' I flapped my arm. 'Just a minor, er, accident.' In the cafeteria, over several cups of tea, we happily swapped several stories. I bitched about my boss, he bitched about his boss. I bitched about the project. He too bitched about the project. I told him how Chhota Don thought that the project was ridiculous; he nodded his head with gusto.

'Each time I uttered the words 'market mapping,' my boss looked ready to shake me within an inch of my life,' The Beaver panted. 'He wanted me to get out and sell fridges — not map markets.'

'I hear you brother,' I nodded commiserating. The Beaver, I noticed, had mellowed down. The shiny, zealous look on his face had disappeared. His face was trying on a new emotion for size: disillusionment. Frankly, I thought it suited him a lot better. I was now convinced that the two of us would get on fabulously. I beamed at him and nodded again. For the next one week, the two of us were inseparable.

ASMs 1 and 2 meted out the same treatment to him as they had (and still did) to me. I was (secretly) delighted. The knowledge that I was no longer the only one being equalled to radioactive waste was exceedingly reassuring. I now had a formal Partner in Pain. I was no longer all by my lonesome. The Beaver, however, was bewildered by their behaviour; and a trifle hurt. 'Just ignore them,' I told him one day from the lofty pedestal of experience. 'They are just a bunch of pompous idiots. Don't let them get to you.'

Chhota Don decided to split the 'faltu' market-mapping project between the two of us. He assigned the West and East zones to The Beaver and the larger North Delhi zone to me. On the upside, that meant that I would now have to map 500 outlets instead of 1000. On the flipside, that meant that after having chased ASMs 1 and 2 in circles, I now had a new ASM to chase: ASM No. 3 aka The Wall. If blatant hostility was the weapon of choice for ASMs 1 and 2, then, blatant non-responsiveness was that of The Wall. So, in the days that followed, I was forced to strike up one-sided conversations with different angles of The Wall's head.

Monday
Me: (To The Wall's right ear) 'Hi there. How are you?'
The Wall (Staring at his screen. No response.)

Tuesday
Me: (To The Wall's left ear) 'Er, can you please take me with you to the market?'
The Wall (Staring at his thumb. No response.)

Wednesday
Me: (To The Wall's left nostril) 'Excuse me, but I need to meet your distributor.'
The Wall (Staring at his shoe. No response.)

Thursday
Me: (To The Wall's receding hairline) 'Look, Boss wants you to take me to the market.'
The Wall (Staring at his wart. No response)

Friday
Me: (To The Wall's weak chin) 'Listen mister, we have to work together. You need to take me to the market.'
The Wall (Staring into space. No response)

Little wonder then that, by the end of the week, I was THIS close to knocking my head against The Wall.

The following Monday morning, after a weekend spent dodging calls from mom between attempts to cook (read: crack an egg open and scramble it), I left for work wondering which object (animate or otherwise) The Wall would choose to stare at that day. As I entered the office, I saw a crowd gathered around The Wall's cubicle. The exclusive ASM huddle, I thought bitterly, walking past them. A collective guffaw escaped from them at that precise moment. Were they laughing at me?

My mouth tightened. *Well, if they are, I don't care.* I defiantly tossed my hair over my shoulders and pointed my nose to the air.

I had almost reached my desk, when I snap-stopped in my tracks. Wait a minute, had my peripheral vision just caught The Beaver standing with them…LAUGHING? I spiralled around to check. God, YES. It was The Beaver! And YES, he was LAUGHING! I goggled at him in disbelief for a moment, then turned around and dropped into my chair, fighting off a wave of jealousy.

Another burst of laughter followed. Was *he* making fun of me now too? I felt a familiar heat around my eyes. The traitor! The betrayal! When the hell had he gone on from being Fellow Unfortunate to One of the Boys? In the last one week, except for the time that we had been in the market, The Beaver and I had hung out together. He had barely spoken to THEM. When had he moved from being US vs. THEM to being BUM CHUMS with THEM?

I switched on the computer and stared at the screen. Why did they all hate me? Was it because I was a girl? Or was it just *me?* A fat tear rolled down my cheek. I wiped it off angrily. I will NOT let them get to me, I swore under my breath. Let's not forget, I AM A RHINO AND I HAVE A THICK SKIN. I began typing fervently, determined to get through the morning without giving in to the Beaver-shaped dark cloud of misery that continued to float all around me.

A few minutes later, when ASMs 1, 2 and The Wall left for the market, The Beaver shambled towards me.

'Hi,' he said tentatively, leaning over my cubicle. *Oh, so NOW he was talking to me, now that THEY had gone!* I ignored him and stared frostily at my screen.

He cleared his throat. 'Er, how was your weekend?' No response from my end. I was still staring at my screen.

'I'm going to the market in some time,' he mumbled, 'What about you?' Still no response. If only The Wall had been here to see me, I thought. He would have been so proud.

'Listen Zoey,' The Beaver began awkwardly, clearing his throat again. He looked as if he were preparing for a parliamentary speech. 'They are our colleagues. We have to try to get along with them. We can't keep behaving like kids in kindergarten. Besides, they are really quite alright once you start getting to know them.'

My fist clenched around the mouse. I remained mutinously mum.

The Beaver looked askance. 'Anyway,' he said wearily, 'has the Boss arrived?'

Twirling around, I tore into him, 'How the hell should I know? Why don't you ask one of your new best friends?'

He looked away and shook his head as if I was some silly, spoilt child who was being particularly difficult. 'They are not bad guys Zoey,' he said. 'We just got talking the other day and—'

'And what? Hit it off? Fell in love?'

'Hey, come on, that's unfair...you just have to make the effort to get to know them, you know.'

'Oh bugger off,' I belted out, turning to glower at my screen.

The Beaver lingered awkwardly for another second, then slunk off. I glared at his receding back. Who the hell did he think he was, anyway? Lecturing me from the smug altar of new-found love. If he wanted to hang out with THEM, he was more than welcome to. In fact, he could charlie off with them all the way to The Bermuda Triangle. Nothing would make me happier.

From: Lara Krishnan <lara.krishnan@see-mail.com>
To: Zoey Verma <zoey.verma@see-mail.com>
Date: August 29, 11:14 AM
Subject: Latest News From Chennai Branch

My boss is the Spawn of Satan. Quite positive he has 666 imprinted
on his head.

From: Zoey Verma <zoey.verma@see-mail.com>
To: Lara Krishnan <lara.krishnan@see-mail.com>
Date: August 29, 11:23 AM
Subject: Latest News From Delhi Branch
The Beaver is the Spawn of Judas. Positively positive he has two
faces.

A few days later, post running out of things to stare at, The Wall
finally deigned to take me to meet his distributor. In a sprawling
godown in North Delhi, behind a long table, the distributor sat
flicking his chubby fingers through a thick wad of hundred-
rupee notes. He looked up sluggishly, as The Wall and I entered.
After a quick round of introductions, The Wall and the
distributor began discussing Fridge Stuff, while I sat listening to
them, chewing my cuticle.

My tummy was beginning to churn. I was feeling hungry.
Coolio had been empty this morning (big surprise) and therefore
my tum was staging an uprising. I sucked it in, while shifting in
my chair, and prayed that it wouldn't growl. But it did. Very
loudly. The Wall flinched. The distributor looked spooked. I
smiled sheepishly at the distributor and rubbed my tummy.
Damn my tummy and damn Coolio. The distributor's bushy
eyebrows knotted together, then he nodded at one of the shop
boys, who I was delighted to see was soon placing a plate of
biscuits on the counter. I looked gratefully at the distributor,
then made such a dive for the plate that I'm surprised my arm

didn't wrench out of its socket. I liked this distributor. He was not shady and he was kind to my tummy. I bit into my biscuit and beamed at him.

Five biscuits and one very milky tea later, I explained my project to him saying that I would need the help of one of his salesmen to take me to the market. The distributor didn't open his gob for a long moment; then he slung his plump hand on the table, moved his head back and called out to the heavens, 'Oh beta Happy, oh zara madam ko market-sharket dikhaiyyo…' My ears flinched and my eyes widened.

Two seconds later, Happy ambled in. A young, gangly Surd, Happy looked like he would rather be watching the cricket match on telly than escorting some wilting woman to the market. Poor Happy. I almost felt sorry for him. He fluttered around near the door for a minute, then with a hmmph, beckoned me to follow him out. I rattled my empty cup on the saucer, waved a bye to the distributor and trotted off after Happy. Out on the street, Happy veered to a halt near his scooter. *Doesn't anyone in Delhi drive a car?* I agonized, regarding the dusty vehicle. Gritting my teeth, I managed to clamber on to the wretched thing behind Happy. A second later, Happy revved up his scooter, and we were off.

Soon, Happy pulled over in some market in North Delhi. I had barely dismounted, when he turned the ignition key and revved up his scooter once again. 'Kahaan ja rahe ho?' I asked him in a swirl of panic. 'Office,' he replied, with a casual shrug. 'Par…par…baaki ke markets?' I begged, looking wild and afraid. He shrugged again, tightening his helmet. A moment later, I stood blinking after him as he disappeared into the crowd.

No Happy? I felt sick. Had I just been dumped in the wilds of North Delhi to fend for myself? If only Scooter-man were here, I thought unhappily. Scooter-man had sweetly taken me to every market in South Delhi. Happy, on the other hand, had only made me unhappy. I turned around dolefully to make my first hit at an outlet.

After several heated hours spent spinning around North Delhi, I headed back wearily to the office in the evening. As I entered the building, I almost collided into The Chester. Now, I hadn't spoken to The Chester since that incident in the pub. The few times that I had seen The Chester since then, I had ensured that we were separated by no less than ten yards (although quite frankly, even the North Pole wouldn't have been far enough). Unfortunately, at that moment, due to lack of adequate space on the staircase landing and lack of prior notice as well, we were separated by not more than ten inches.

'Hi,' The Chester said. He was smiling at me, rather weirdly.

I rapidly donned the expression of someone who had just swallowed toddy.

'Where have you been?' he crooned. 'I haven't seen you for days!'

I glared at him. *Was he really going to pretend that 'that incident' hadn't happened?*

'Yaar, the other day I was just joking yaar…I don't know why you got so angry.'

My eyes narrowed into slits. Just joking, my foot.

'Come on yaar,' he said. 'It was just a joke.'

My right palm began to twitch. Just a joke, my ass.

'Accha, do you want to go for coffee later?' he breezed.

I blinked at him in disbelief. The nerve of him!

'I should be free by 6. What about you? When can we meet?'

I took a deep breath, then peeped at my watch. 'How

about...' I began...(The Chester looked hopeful)...'Hum... haw...' ...(The Chester waited, breathless)...'Ah, yes I can meet you...' ...(The Chester was now on tenterhooks)... 'NEVER,' I finished off in a yell. 'N-E-V-E-R,' I punctuated for good measure. Then I fired him a mother-of-all-dirty-looks, pirouetted on my heel and nipped off. Seriously! The guy was the pits! How could he be so obtuse? Which animal's skin from which jungle did he have on? I wanted to know. I wanted it too. I thought I had sprouted a thick skin, but really, The Chester beat me hollow.

Back at my terminal, I furiously punched my keyboard, picturing The Chester's face in every key. I had punched The Chester's face for the 99th time when my phone buzzed on the table. It was a text from an unidentifiable number:

HELLOJI. MYSELF RAJ. LIKE FROM DDLJ. HEHE. JUST JOKEING. UR RESPECTFUL MOTHER GIVEN ME UR NUMBER. WANT 2 MEET FOR MOVIE. U AND ME?

I fumed at the message, eyes shining with madness. Then I rammed DELETE so hard that my finger almost broke off. The Beaver chose that moment to rear his two-faced head over my cubicle.

'Hi,' he began anxiously. I fired him a fierce look.

'Erm, I need to talk to you...' he whispered, clearing his throat.

'You don't want to talk to me right now,' I ground out. 'I am in a foul mood.'

'Er, oh, okay...' he said. A pause, then, 'want to talk about it?'

'No,' I yelped, then resumed punching my keyboard wildly.

The Beaver didn't take the hint. He continued to stick around.

I ignored him for a whole quarter of a minute before gnashing, 'What do you want?'

He cleared his throat again. 'Er, actually, I had to convey some news to you.'

I looked up irritably from my screen. 'What news?'

He looked shaky. 'Well, um, you see, Boss told me to tell you that after you map the North zone, you will have to map the West zone too.'

'Why?' I said, staring at him. 'You are supposed to do that.'

The Beaver bore my scrutiny uneasily, shuffling his feet like a baby elephant. 'Er, actually, I am being taken off the project.'

'Oh. Why?' Was he getting fired? HAH!

He scratched his oily nose, looking uncomfortable. 'Because I am being given a sales territory to handle.'

'You are what?' I spat out, incredulous.

'Well, you see,' The Beaver rushed on, 'Boss thinks that I am ready to handle sales for a territory. I will finish mapping the East zone, of course, but you will have to do the…'

'What about me?' I caterwauled. 'Why aren't I being given a territory?'

The Beaver held up his hands, looking tormented. 'I don't know. You will have to ask Boss.'

I pounced. 'You're damn right I will.'

Soon after that, I knocked on Chhota Don's cabin door. Okay, so I wasn't exactly dying to go out there and sell fridges, but if Chhota Don thought that The Beaver was ready to do it, then I was ready to do it too.

'Come in,' Chhota Don roared.

I stamped in as if I were marching into battle. Chhota Don's scruffy head was bent over some documents. I loomed over his table and cleared my throat. 'Sir,' I began, sounding all loud and defiant. A few words down, however, my anger, jealousy and self-pity suddenly merged together and, to my utter chagrin, my voice began to shake. 'So Sir,' I whimpered, 'Is he really getting a territory?'

Chhota Don appraised me for a moment. Then he nodded his head, 'Yes, he is. I have been wanting to talk to you about that…but you were nowhere to be seen. I never know where you are half the time.'

'I was in the market, Sir,' I replied wearily.

'I hope so,' he snapped, as if he half suspected that I had been napping at home instead. As if I would nap at home in the middle of a working day. Erm okay, I might have done that once. But that was all. Just once. Erm, okay, twice actually. Ahem, three times to be precise, oh all right six times then; but only because it was so HOT outside. 80 degrees Celsius at least.

'Anyway,' Chhota Don continued, 'you will also have to map the West zone now…that boy will finish East Delhi before he starts handling his territory.'

'But Sir, when will I be given a territory?'

Chhota Don leaned back in his chair, clasped his hands and watched me meditatively. I could see that he was mentally running a Sales Manager Material Checklist on me.

- Can she become Best Friends Forever with B-grade-Bollywood-luvin' Shady Singh? (No)
- Can she, over a glass of 'orangish-looking' alcohol, talk to him about 'gori chamdi' from Bangkok? (No)
- Importantly, can she sell fridges to him? (No. Not even with the help of feminine wiles? No. Because she has about as many of those as a DTC bus.)

Chhota Don may as well have sadistically waved the Checklist in my face and announced that I was poster child for

'Anything but Sales Manager Material,' because his next words were, 'you are not ready yet.'

'I'm not?' I croaked, leaning forward in my chair.

'Not yet,' he said, scrutinizing my face. A pause followed, then he took in a deep breath, 'Zoey, are you sure you really want to be in sales?'

I blinked at him. Was he indirectly hinting that I should quit?

Suddenly I wanted to burst into tears. My rhino-like skin crumbled along with the remaining 'Five Habits of Highly Successful People'. I now felt utterly unsuccessful and totally worthless. I was no longer Super Woman—just a timid, little, she-mouse.

'Well, are you?' Chhota Don impatiently prodded.

'Yes Sir,' I mumbled feebly, 'I am…um sure.' Was I sure? Of course, I wasn't. I wasn't sure of anything. What was the point of anything anyway? What was the point of me?

'Hmm, okay, we'll see,' Chhota Don said, running agitated fingers through his hair. 'For now, please finish your project.'

I nodded crestfallen, then walked out shakily from his cabin. Twenty-five minutes later, I sat addled and limp in an auto. I hadn't been able to concentrate on work, I was so disturbed. The question, *Do you really want to be in sales?* kept whipping around in my head. The fattest imaginable testimony to my inadequacy as a working professional. I leaned back in my seat, my head in my hands. Did I really want to do this job? I had no idea. All I knew was that I often found myself envying other people for the jobs they had:

- Like Chhota Don's driver, who, out of a ten-hour shift, 'worked' for one and a half hours and napped for the remaining eight and a half.

- Or the Security Guard, who spent his day chit-chatting with his buddies, reading five different newspapers and occasionally throwing out dodgy visitors.
- Or the Cafeteria boy, who drifted to and fro with a tray of cups and whose only source of stress was remembering the ratio of tea to coffee drinkers in a board room.
- Or the receptionist who left daily on the dot of 5 p.m. after a 'hectic' schedule of back-to-back smiles and hellos.

Now if only those jobs had more attractive salaries, I thought with a moan. I pulled out my phone from my bag and checked my messages. The Ex's 'thinking about you' message still sat in my inbox. I had not replied to him then because somehow I had drudged up the will to pay heed to A) the warnings clanging in my head and B) the warnings reverberating from Lara.

But as I sat in the auto, the words of Chhota Don still booming in my head, those warnings seemed like faint, distant echoes. I was suddenly feeling weak. And whiny and clingy. So whiny and clingy that, before I knew it, I was calling up The Ex, aka Velcro Man. The man I had dumped for being *so* whiny and clingy.

7

I was wallowing in a deep sea of self-pity. Chhota Don was convinced that I was a shiny prototype for Waste of Space. The Beaver had ditched me for cooler friends who still regarded me as radioactive waste. In the absence of scooters, I was travelling by autos, whose drivers were deliberately doing a 'Dilli Darshan' on me. Oh, and the cheeriest part of my existence (apart from Coolio) was The Velcro Man, who hadn't stopped whining since we had gotten back together.

In hindsight, I should have paid heed to that article in Cosmo magazine on 'Ten Reasons Why You Shouldn't Get Back Together With Your Ex'. In particular, I should have paid attention to Reason No. 1: *When the rush of getting back together with your Ex wears off, so will your amnesia; and you will remember exactly why you had dumped him in the first place.* Now, of course, I had known why I had dumped The Velcro Man, even on that fateful day a week ago when my weak self had called him up; but it wasn't until after sixty minutes of getting back together with him that same day, that I *truly remembered* why I had dumped him.

That Fateful Day A Week Ago:
8.07 p.m. (after several minutes of whispering sweet nothings and mushy somethings into the phone), Velcro Man and I

decide to get back together (I am euphoric. I now have a familiar shoulder to cry on.)

8.08 p.m.: I ask Velcro Man how Bangalore has been treating him. (FYI, Velcro Man works in an IT company in Bangalore). 'Oh Bangalore,' Velcro Man grumbles, 'It's okay, but the traffic, ugh, don't even get me started...'

8.21 p.m.: Velcro Man is still grumbling about the traffic in Bangalore. I now know enough about the traffic in Bangalore to apply for the job of a traffic cop in that city. 'Anyway,' I say, changing the subject, 'How is your job going?' Velcro Man pauses, then, 'Where do I start? Firstly, I get paid peanuts...' (FYI, Velcro Man is amongst the highest paid in our batch) '...my salary is so measly...'

8.37 p.m.: Velcro Man is still whining about how measly his salary is. 'So, anyway,' I interject sharply, 'about my job...' We have spoken about HIM from the word go. I am now determined to talk about ME, but...

At 8.38 p.m., it is Velcro Man who is talking; because we are back on the magnificent subject of HIM.

8.51 p.m.: Velcro Man is still talking, '...and my boss,' he whines, 'oof, don't even get me started...' Before he does get started on his boss, I cut him off with a loud shriek 'DO YOU KNOW, MY BOSS THINKS I'M A JOKER?' There is a pause. Velcro Man is side-tracked, but only for a second, 'Oh, does he?' he says, before hopping right back on track, 'but MY boss...oofho...where do I get started...'

9.05 p.m.: Velcro Man is still WHINING about his boss.

9.06 p.m.: My initial euphoria of getting back with him vanishes.

9.06 p.m. (and 40 seconds): My amnesia vanishes too.

9.07 p.m.: I say to myself: Aaahh!…so THAT'S why I had dumped him.

A week later, I was still doing the long-distance-relationship thing with Velcro Man. I knew I should have re-dumped him; but I hadn't gotten around to doing it. Six months ago, when I had told him that I no longer wanted to see him, he had looked at me as if I had morphed into an alien. In the weeks that followed, I had communicated to him that we were over, in various ways—in person, over the phone, via text, on a Post-it. But Velcro Man refused to take the hint. After all, how could he (Third-Ranker-from-Top-and-Sort-Of-Cute) get dumped by me (Third-Ranker-from-Bottom-and-Sort-of-Giraffe-like)? We followed a pattern in the days that followed: I ran, he clung. I shouted, 'It's over!' He shouted, 'P.M.S!' Finally, after twenty-three days of communicating to him (in person, over the phone, via text, on a Post-it) that it wasn't P.M.S, Velcro Man got the message.

But now (because I was weak and a fool), here we were, back to square one, and I, quite frankly, didn't have the energy to move out of it just yet.

Meanwhile, things at work continued to be difficult. The Beaver and the other ASMs had become best buddies; The Beaver had begun handling a territory and he and I were barely speaking.

Relief came in small measure, a week later, with the news of a two-day National Annual Sales conference in Jaipur. Now, I was not exactly looking forward to being stuck with a group of 100 fridge salesmen (I mean, I could barely handle the few lurking in my office), but I was really looking forward to meeting Lara. I was looking forward to meeting my one and only true Ally in Angst.

On a Friday morning, at an ungodly hour, I boarded the first flight to Jaipur. We had been given two flight options, and I — with the fervent intention of avoiding being stuck with Chhota Don and his crew on the same flight — opted for the earlier (red-eye) flight instead. The way I saw it — In-home Lack of Sleep was infinitely preferable to In-flight Cold Shoulder Treatment.

A few hours later, I stood in the lobby of a plush hotel, waiting to be allotted my room number. Lara, I had learnt from the lady at the reception, had not yet arrived. I was just being handed my room key, when I spotted Wimp-eater sauntering into the lobby, luggage in tow. I bagged my key and ducked behind the nearest potted plant for cover. The last place I wanted to be was in Wimp-eater's line of vision. Unfortunately, I remained well within his sight because the potted plant was all of two feet tall, while I was a near six. I looked around wildly for taller objects to hide behind. Ah, a pillar!

I was just about to make a lunge for it, when someone rent the air with my name from behind. Astonished, I wheeled around to find that 'someone' charging at me like a crazed bull. For a second, I froze; then realized that that 'someone' was Lara! Without warning, she dropped her bags and bear-hugged me as if she was seeing me after ten years spent on Mars. I hugged her back, then disentangled myself quickly and looked over my shoulder. Phew. Wimp-eater had left the lobby. Thank God! I could now freely indulge my excitement at seeing Lara.

'You look washed out,' I heard Lara yelp. She was scanning my tired eyes and bony frame.

'And you look like the undead,' I remarked in alarm, noticing her dark circles and sallow face. As we trundled towards our rooms, Lara began a deluge about just how bad things had been for her at the Chennai office.

'It's been more than two months and yet they treat me like a social reject!' she mewled. 'They all have more experience than I do and they are making sure I know it.'

'You're telling me?' I mumbled, as I reached my room. 'Things are so bad at the Delhi Branch, that I have gotten back t…' I broke off. I was about to babble that I had started seeing Velcro Man, but had stopped myself just in time. I knew that Lara would not take the news well (according to her, Velcro Man was a self-centred pig and for the life of her couldn't fathom why I had hooked up with him in the first place); and so, there was clearly no point telling her about the re-hook-up. Besides, it was just a temporary situation. I intended to break up with Velcro Man soon enough.

But I had forgotten how NOSY Lara could be. FYI, Lara can be very NOSY. So NOSY, that she'd give Poirot a run for his money.

We were sitting in my room, sipping tea (our conference was not to start for another hour and forty-five minutes), when she casually asked, 'What were you going to say back in the corridor?' (Lara's Nosiness: Proof Exhibit No 1).

'What do you mean?' I asked, deliberately playing dumb.

'You said you had gotten back…then you stopped short…'

'Um, really?' I mumbled cagily. 'Is that what I said?'

'Yes, Zoey, that is what you said. So I repeat, gotten back what?' (Lara's Nosiness: Proof Exhibit No 2).

'Erm, I don't remember,' I hedged. 'It probably wasn't important.'

'Are you sure?' Lara asked. She was looking at me oddly. 'It sounded kind of important.' (Lara's Nosiness: Proof Exhibit No 3).

'Oh,' I flapped a dismissive arm, 'I was probably just going to say that I've gotten-erm-gone back to travelling by autos. The North Delhi salesman is not as cooperative as Scooter-man was, you know.'

She slung me a dubious look. Then out of nowhere, she quizzed, 'How is Velcro Man?' (Lara's Nosiness: Proof Exhibit No 4).

'V-velcro Man?' I faltered. 'How would I know? I'm not in touch with him.' I felt my nose grow an inch.

'So you never replied to his message?' (Lara's Nosiness: Proof Exhibit No 5).

'No, I didn't,' I lied, pressing the tip of my nose.

'Hmm, so how come there's a rumour going around that *you have gotten back together with* him?!' (Lara's Nosiness: Proof Exhibit No 6).

I blinked at her, my face burning with guilt. How on earth had the rumour reached Lara? What had Velcro Man used? Jungle drums? I was *so* going to get him for this.

Lara was now outfacing me, fists on hips. 'Er, um...' I incoherently mumbled, refusing to meet her eye.

'Tell all, right now. Leave out nothing.' (Lara's Nosiness: Proof Exhibit No 7).

I sank, defeated, in my chair and let the words stream out of my mouth in a torrent, 'Beaver ditched me for THEM...He got a territory...I didn't...I'm not good enough...Chhota Don said so...was feeling like a dork...AND totally worthless...also very clingy...called up Velcro Man...very stupid of me...back together now...he is still whining...it's only temporary...need to dump him soon...'

I stopped mid-torrent, trying to decide whether the peculiar sound that had erupted from Lara had been a grunt or a choke.

'The man is a wimp,' Lara hit out, 'I don't know how you ever went out with him.'

'How did you ever go out with him?' she demanded in the next instant. (Lara's Nosiness: Proof Exhibit No 8). (See? N-O-S-Y. What did I tell you? And thanks to her nosiness I was now feeling a zillion times worse about the re-hook-up than I already had.).

'Don't ask,' I whinged, then miserably added, 'I guess wimps of a feather flock together...'

That evening, after a series of boring, back-to-back sales presentations, everyone gathered in the ballroom for the much-awaited party. With lights flashing, music blaring, and alcohol flowing, the room soon buzzed with a frenzied energy. Lara and I stood in a corner and watched with some alarm as a hundred sales men glutted whisky like water, gyrated to Bollywood 'item numbers,' and boisterously back-slapped each other. Feeling overwhelmed, I held on to Lara's arm. A few feet from me, I could see The Beaver jigging his legs amongst ASMs 1 to 4, who in turn were hooting and whistling. Not too far from him, Chhota Don was boogieing around Wimp-eater who was perusing all his flock with glazed eyes and a drunken smile.

'Having a good time?' a voice asked us from behind. Lara and I looked up to find The Schmoozer, leaning against the wall, looking smug. I hadn't seen that smug face in over two months. (Not that I had missed it. I hadn't. Not one bit. And judging from Lara's expression, neither had she.)

'Well?' The Schmoozer prodded. Lara shrugged her left shoulder in response. I shrugged my right. Not satisfied with the coordinated shrugs, he prodded again, 'Enjoying your first sales conference?'

'Yes, we are,' Lara finally snapped. 'So much so that we're hoping it's our last.'

In the days following the conference, things began to take a turn for the worse; and my self-pity slowly began to make way for pure, unadulterated rage. There were several triggers that caused this development; the first of which, I absolutely did not see coming. I had just begun mapping the East zone and was roaming around one afternoon, in some East Delhi market, when I got a call from Scooter-man. (It was one of those friendly 'What's up? How's life?' type calls.) I told him despondently that nothing was up, it was all down and that life pretty much sucked.

Soon I was illuminating him on the why. I'd had a tough time covering the North markets, I uttered. Was having a tougher time covering the East markets, I snivelled. All because, the East Delhi salesman (like Happy) had refused to take me with him on his scooter. Scooter-man responded sweetly, 'Koi baat nahin. I will take you to the East wale markets on *my* scooter.' 'You'll take me on *your* scooter?' I blinked. Meaning no more horrible autos? I was thrilled. I clapped my hands and let out a whoop, then spent some time welling out my heartfelt thanks to Scooter-man.

That evening, I gushed about Scooter-man's magnanimous gesture to Lara. Lara sounded less thrilled, more sceptical.

'Why would he do that?' her voice trilled down the phone.

'I don't know,' I replied. 'I guess he is just being nice.'

'Nice?' she mocked. 'Yeah, right. Who is nice for the heck of it anymore?' I suppressed a stab of annoyance. Did Lara always have to be such a wet blanket?

The next morning, sharp at 10.30 a.m., I arrived at the designated meeting spot (a bus stop in South Delhi). In a short while Scooter-man appeared, in an unexpected tidal wave of heavy perfume. I fell back, befogged from the assault. It seemed that somewhere between the last time I rode on Scooter-man's steed and now, the man had dunked himself in a tank full of cologne. And what was up with his hair? It looked unusually black; come to think of it, so did his sideburns. Had he used dye??? And wait, had Scooter-man put on make up? I twisted my neck to peer into his face. No, that was just powder—three fat layers of it. Scooter-man was now grinning at me broadly. I gave him a weak smile and scrambled on to the scooter behind him. Palm pressed against my nose, I stared at his dyed hair. What on earth had triggered this drastic makeover? A niggling suspicion was beginning to take seed in my mind. Had Lara been right in doubting Scooter-man's motives after all? *Oh God, please let her not be right.*

But as the day wore on, and the usually reticent Scooter-man shone me a smile here, dashed me a wink there, insisted on treating me to hot pakodas, then insisted on dropping me home, the seed of suspicion began to sprout into a plant. But it wasn't until later, when upon reaching my building, Scooter-man pulled off his helmet and asked *if I was 'alone' at home and could he come up for a cup of 'chai'*, did that plant burgeon into a full scale Banyan tree. The writing was now clear on the wall. Dumb CLUELESS Me! Why couldn't I have seen what Lara had known then?? Scooter-man was trying to make a move on me, and he had come armed with perfume, powder and a pack of hair dye. I was so mad, I wanted to *spit.* I scrambled off the scooter, snatched up my bag to my shoulder, and told him in no uncertain terms that he wasn't getting *any* 'chai' and that he could go straight down to hell. With that, I spun around and trooped off, but not before catching a glimpse of Scooter-man, morosely mopping the layers off his face.

The second trigger accelerating my flight to Angerville, followed close on the heels of the Scooter-man fracas. I was in office on a Wednesday evening, quietly updating my status report, when Chhota Don called me into his cabin. There, he proceeded to inform me (most patronizingly) that *because* I had nearly finished my project and *because* he didn't know what else to do with me, he was giving me a territory to manage. I suppose I should have felt grateful. But I didn't. Not one bit. There had been one too many 'becauses' in Chhota Don's statement. I was deliberately being humiliated and, quite frankly, my pride (not to mention, self esteem) was sick of all the blows.

Perhaps, the only person more furious than I was, was ASM No. 1 because A) I was now to handle part of his territory and B) Over the next two weeks, I was to tail him *and* observe him on the job.

And so, not surprisingly, over the next few days, ASM No. 1 zealously dealt out every trick known to man to throw me off his tail.

Trick 1: The 'You Heard Wrong' trick

This trick involves ASM No. 1 telling me to meet him in say, market A, where he doesn't show up, because apparently I heard wrong and was, in fact, supposed to meet him in market B.

Trick 2: The 'I Forgot To Tell You' trick

This trick involves ASM No. 1 telling me to meet him at say, Dealer A's store, where he doesn't show up, because apparently he forgot to tell me that there was a change of plan and that I was to meet him at Dealer B's store instead.

Trick 3: The 'I'm On Holiday' trick

This trick involves ASM No. 1 telling me that he is on holiday and hence will not be going to the market that day when in fact, he is not on holiday and very much in the market that day.

For seven days, I was shafted by ASM No. 1 at every turn. (In that period I walloped a lot of rage; huge instalments, in fact, on the road to ulcerdom). Mercifully, by the eighth day, ASM No.1 had exhausted his little bag of tricks and so, that morning, to my utter amazement, I found him exactly where he'd told me he would be: outside Shady Singh's store. I wish I could say that I was thrilled, but it turned out, I wasn't. It had suddenly hit me that of all the distributors in the entire town, *in the entire world*, I would now have to service the one distributor whom I simply couldn't stand.

Shortly, inside the store, I sat watching ASM No. 1 grovel on his knees begging Shady Singh to buy a new range of our refrigerators. Shady Singh looked bored. He was convinced that this new range was trash. ASM No. 1 continued to grovel. With targets to meet, he was beginning to look desperate. This is fun, I thought, watching him. I was enjoying myself. I even had a whole muhahahaha-type evil laugh reverberating in my head.

It took a couple of minutes, perhaps even a whole quarter of an hour, for it to occur to me that pretty soon I would be in exactly the same position as ASM No.1 was in now: on all fours, trying to peddle some poor fridge. I suddenly felt vacuous. My heart started palpitating. I nearly blacked out on my stool. When I wobbled back to the present (after a pretty long spell), it was to find Shady Singh peering at me, 'Madam,' he said condescendingly, patting his shining bald pate, 'aap is job mein kya kar rahi hain? Aapko is job mein nahin hona chahiye.' My face coloured and my jaw clenched. Palpitations flew out the window. I was back to feeling ballistic.

Later that afternoon, as I got ready to clamber on to ASM No. 1's scooter, he turned around and said, 'I hope you are planning to buy your own two-wheeler. You are going to need it soon. I am not your driver, you know.' I blinked at him tremulously. *Buy a two-wheeler? But-but...I don't know how to ride one!*

I rounded on The Beaver that evening (temporarily forgetting that I was still cheesed off with him) and asked, with fevered eyes, what I should do about the whole 'two-wheeler' situation given my lack of balancing skills. 'But didn't they ask you whether you could ride a two-wheeler at the interview?' The Beaver frowned.

'Yes, they did,' I mumbled.

'What did you say?' he asked daftly.

'I lied,' I told him, defiant. The Beaver shook his head as if he didn't approve.

Really, he was most annoying. Why had I even bothered to talk to him?

Desperate, I turned to my next port of call—Velcro Man. 'I can't ride a scooter,' I yammered to him that evening over the phone. 'What am I going to dooo?' But soon enough, one whole minute of talking about me, and my scooter situation, had started making Velcro Man restive. I had monopolized the conversation long enough. It was time for him to take control. 'You are going on about some *scooter*,' he derided, tone accusing, 'wait till you hear about my car!'

I'm not sure how long I spent listening to Velcro Man ramble about the millimetre-long scratch on his Honda City, but let me assure you, I was kicking myself for having called him up, the W H O L E time.

If the week had been bad, the weekend proved to be worse, because I was graced by the visit of an unexpected guest: Throbbing Toothache.

Now, honestly, my tooth had been aching on and off for the past six months. But I had been avoiding going to the dentist, because let's face it — a trip to a dentist is just about as much fun as, well, a trip to a dentist. But that weekend, my toothache inevitably reached its 'cannot-avoid-a-dental-appointment-anymore' peak. And so the following Monday, head heavy from not having slept for two consecutive nights, I ended up dragging myself to a clinic. An hour-long wait later, I nervously sat in the dreaded chair, my mouth wide open.

The dentist (an old-ish, rather bored looking man) leaned over to take a look. 'Good God,' he exploded, swaying back. 'Why on earth didn't you come earlier?'

I turned a sheepish-red. 'I don't know,' I said miserably.

'Your teeth require a lot of work,' he carped.

'Teeth?' I parroted. 'As in plural of tooth? As in more than one tooth?' I asked dimly.

'Yes,' he replied shortly, looking at me as though my brain needed a 'lot of work' too.

'But just one tooth is aching,' I said, frantic.

He whistled in pique.

'Okay,' I said impassively, 'how many teeth? And what kind of work?'

'Let me take an x-ray of your jaw first and then I will be able to explain,' he said. About half an hour later, the two of us stared at the x-ray. He then pointed to one…two…three teeth, shaking his head, each time. Teeth-pointing and head-shaking over, he briskly rattled off the words — *root canal* and *dental implants*. Now, root canal, I had had the misfortune of having been intimate with earlier. But what *ever* was a dental implant, I thought in a tizzy.

I voiced the question in a muted tone.

'Well,' said the dentist, 'unlike a root canal, in the case of a dental implant, I will have to extract the whole tooth, not just part of it. I will then have to do a surgery to drill a hole in your jaw and implant a false tooth.'

'Good lord,' I gasped.

'And let me warn you,' he ruthlessly continued, 'dental implants are expensive.'

'How expensive?' I dared to ask.

He mentioned an amount. I blinked at him, stuffed my little finger into my ear and shook it vigorously. I was beginning to think that my ears needed a 'lot of work' too.

'Come again?' I asked, having shaken my little finger, till it hurt.

He repeated the same *unholy, obscene* amount.

'Are you alright?' he asked a moment later, scrutinizing my ashen face.

'Barely,' I mumbled shakily.

'Hmm,' he said—then added, 'of course, that amount was just the cost of the dental implant. You also have the root canal to think of,' he said. *Great. The crap just keeps-a-coming.*

'What if I just got all my teeth extracted and got dentures instead?' I asked hopefully. 'Wouldn't that be cheaper?'

'I'm not sure. I'll have to get back to you on that,' he said. Then he proceeded to sanctimoniously rub the proverbial salt on my wounds. 'If you had taken better care of your teeth, it would not have come to this,' he said.

Oh shut up, I thought. I mean what was he going on about anyway? He ought to be smiling and putting a garland around my neck. I was, after all, his walking lottery ticket.

Later, as I walked out of the clinic (with a newly acquired companion: Massive Headache), I couldn't help but brood on that unholy, obscene amount. My birthday was a few months away and I had been scrounging and saving for a tablet to gift to myself. No way was I going to be able to buy it now. I slouched out of the clinic, contemplating boarding a bus instead of an auto, what with my looming bankruptcy. Just as I stepped out of the compound, my cell phone beeped. I scrambled around in my bag and yanked it out. Message from a familiar, yet unidentifiable number:

HELLOJI. THIS SIDE RAJ. REMEMBER I SMS U. Y U NOT REPLY? REPLY SOON. M WAITING 4 U.

I felt like dashing the brains out of my phone. I was sorely tempted to march home and stick my head inside Coolio to cool off. I had had ENOUGH.

It was little surprise then, that when a moment later my cell phone began ringing, I was forced to clamp it as hard as I could against the full jet of steam hissing out of my ear. It was Chhota Don yelling at me to rush to office ASAP. I decided, right then, that if he chucked any more crap my way, I would take the words *I* and *QUIT* and ram them down his throat.

Forty-five minutes later, face pinched with rage, I marched into Chhota Don's cabin.

'You wanted to see me?' I asked waspishly, lowering over his table.

'Yes, sit down,' he said, looking up from his screen.

Fists clenched, I plunged down and geared myself up for More Crap.

'I have just been speaking to HR…' he began.

I gripped my chair, half-rising. *You have been speaking to HR??? You have been speaking to them about firing me? YOU don't get to fire me. BECAUSE I QUIT.* I was just about to fling those words at Chhota Don, when I heard him say, 'One of your batchmates…' (he took a name)…'has put in his papers…'

I blinked in astonishment, flopping back in my seat. My first thought: *So you're not firing me?!* My second thought: *The Schmoozer has put in his papers??!*

But if news of A) me still having a job and B) The Schmoozer quitting, had caught my anger off-guard, then Chhota Don's next words kicked it right out of my system.

'You have been asked to take his place, Zoey. You will be moving to Mumbai Head Office by the end of this month.'

8

Hurrah! I was going to Mumbai! When Chhota Don had
uttered those magical words, I had had to sit on my hands to
stop myself from flinging them around his neck. I had been so
thrilled; I'd thought I'd blow up with the current of joy running
through me.

I still couldn't believe it. No more Chhota Don. No more
ASMs 1 to 4. No more Shady Singh. The very thought had me
dancing in circles. And perhaps, because of it, my hostility
towards them all vanished almost overnight. In its place there
now floated a new-found Gandhian-like feeling of Zen. Thus,
much to their amazement, I had been throwing them big,
broad beaming smiles (because I was deliriously happy and
they, poor souls, knew not what they were doing).

- 20 days to departure, ASM No. 1 throws me nth+1 Dirty
  Looks. Me: Big Broad beaming smile
- 15 days to departure, Shady Singh gives me nth+1 Shady
  Looks. Me: Big Broad beaming smile
- 10 days to departure, The Chester gives me nth+1 Slimy
  Looks. Me: Big Broad beaming smile

- 3 days to departure, nth+1 auto driver deliberately does 'Dilli Darshan' on me and charges astronomically high fare. Me: Big Broad beaming smile.

When the day of my departure arrived, no one was sorry to see me go, except A) my landlord who was still threatening to Bluedart his son's photo to my folks and B) Coolio, until I promised it that I would lug it back to Mumbai with me. The Beaver's reaction I wasn't quite able to peg, but as I cleared my desk that evening and caught him wafting around near my cubicle, I had a faint notion that he was feeling a mite wistful, perhaps, even a little envious.

'It's really great that you are going to the H.O,' he said, ruminatively, watching me pitch a whole stack of unfilled questionnaires into the bin. I nodded, and paused to wonder why The Schmoozer had quit in the first place. Had he been asked to quit? Hah. Highly unlikely. More likely he had found a more notable prey from a more notable company to schmooze. But for once, I wasn't grouching. In fact, I decided I might even send him a cheery 'Best of Luck' text.

'You will get a chance to interact and work with all the top bosses now,' The Beaver added.

I looked up from the fresh stack in my hands, flabbergasted. Top bosses? Bugger. For one unholy second, I imagined a dark, ominous Wimp-eater shaped cloud looming over me, then speedily dismissed the image. I was going to Mumbai. I was happy. And nothing, not even the prospect of Wimp-eater was going to rain on my parade. 'Thanks,' I replied, before producing my by-now legendary big, broad, beaming smile.

In the face of my hundred-watter, The Beaver looked fazed for a second, then he leaned forward and eagerly whispered, 'No hard feelings then?'

I pondered that one for a bit. 'None,' I eventually said. I meant it too. Then I collected my bag, picked up my box and sailed out of the door without a backward look.

That weekend, before starting work at the Mumbai Head Office, I paid a visit to my folks in Pune on the insistence of my mom; she hadn't seen me for all of three months now. Perhaps, the only person more relieved than me about my transfer to Mumbai, was my mom.

'You have become SO thin!!!' were her first words as soon as she opened the door. Her voice was at least ten octaves higher than usual and she was inspecting me from top to bottom as if I were a performing flea. 'Have you been eating properly?' she torpedoed.

'Hi to you too, mom,' I said, walking past her, dragging my luggage behind me. My dad was reading a newspaper in a secluded corner of the hall. I went over to him and dropped a kiss on his soft, balding head. 'Good to see you,' he said with the glimmer of a smile, sticking his head out from behind his newspaper only to duck back immediately after.

Mom had now marched into the hall and had started yelling. 'I should never have sent you to Delhi. Look at you. So thin. So pale. You look like a scarecrow. God knows what you have been eating...or not eating...I will have to fatten you up...Now that you are going to be in Mumbai, you better come here every weekend!' Then she turned around and sashayed into the kitchen.

Dad and I exchanged glances. He smiled. I gritted my teeth.

'Lunch is ready,' she hollered from within. 'I have made parathas.'

I moved towards the dining table and lunged into a chair. In the next few minutes, she slapped down three heavily-buttered parathas onto my plate, in rapid succession.

'When do you start work in Mumbai?' she asked a while later, as I tried to force down the last of the three.

'Monday,' I mumbled, massaging my tummy (which having shrunk in Delhi was now groaning from this sudden attack).

'I think they are making you work too hard,' she griped, 'so skinny you have become.' Then she swished back into the kitchen and marched out with...*christ*...yet another heavily-buttered paratha.

'I can't have that, mom! I'm full!' I protested.

'What full? Eat!' she ordered, standing over me, hands on her hips.

I exhaled. What was it with moms and their uncontrollable desire to stuff their offspring?

I was practically choking on Heavily-buttered Paratha No. 4, when she sat down at the table. 'Sabina aunty had called last night,' she said.

'Uh-huh,' I managed to wring out. Sabina Aunty was my mom's cousin and her partner in melodrama.

'Her daughter is getting married,' she said.

'Oh okay,' I mumbled, then added with a frown, 'but isn't she really young? I...'

'Just six months younger than you,' my mom interrupted. 'She is marrying a really nice boy. They found him on the internet...'

Bugger. Suddenly I knew where this conversation was headed.

'I got a call from the mother of that other nice boy,' I heard her say. 'She said that her son had contacted you but that you hadn't bothered to reply. She was not happy.'

I noticed that my mom didn't look happy either.

'Why didn't you meet him?' she accused. 'He was in Delhi at that time.'

'I didn't have time,' I bleated.

'Hmmph,' she scoffed. 'Anyway, you can meet him now. He is back in Mumbai.'

'Let her be,' my dad said firmly, looking up from his newspaper. 'She has just come back. Give her some time to settle down in her job.'

I threw him a grateful look.

'Settle?' my mom huffed. 'Yes. It is time for her to settle. It is time for her to settle with a good boy. But she doesn't want to meet any good boy. She is stubborn, just like you.' Dad scowled, then in a flash, buried his head back into his newspaper. Mom, meanwhile had rounded on me. 'Do you think good boys grow on trees?' she ranted, flapping her arms; then without waiting for me to answer, flounced back into the kitchen. When she came out, a minute later, she was waving Heavily-buttered Paratha No.5. I closed my eyes in pain. Bad enough to have to listen to all this talk of 'settling'; add to that, this Paratha-thon. No wonder, I was feeling nauseous.

I realized with a slightly heavy heart, that it was time to set the record straight with my mom. It was a daunting prospect, but I felt compelled to tell her that I refused to marry for the next three years. At the very least. I had a sudden vision of her chasing me with her rolling pin at the heels of that announcement, and quickly glanced at the main door. Exit Route just three feet away. Thank God.

'Er...mom,' I croaked, sights fixed on Exit Route, 'there's something you should know...'

'What?' my mom's voice broke. Then, noticing my flushed face, she struck, 'You have met someone, haven't you? That's the reason you didn't meet that nice boy in Delhi, isn't it? Who is he? Is he a nice boy? How much does he earn? Is he a good boy? Is he...'

I shook my head. Okay, so I was seeing Velcro Man, but that was information my mom didn't need to know. Besides, it was just a temporary technicality. She hadn't registered my head-shake because she was still in her own groove, 'Is he from the same caste? Is he from a good family? Is he...'

I shook my head again, this time a little more vigorously. She finally caught the movement and stopped. 'You mean he is not of the same caste?' she queried incredulously.

'No, I mean I haven't met anyone. It's not that,' I said peeved.

'Oofff...What is it then?' she asked.

'I don't want to see any more boys for now, I do not want to get married for another three years at least.' There, it was done. I sat, holding my breath...

My mom stood speechless for a second; then a warbling sound and a dramatic flutter of hand coming to rest on her heart. 'Three years?' she whispered.

'Yes,' I said firmly. 'Three years.'

Mom now looked like she was about to wilt down to the floor. I looked beseechingly at my dad. His head was still buried in a newspaper.

'But what are you going to do for three years?' my mom asked wanly.

'Erm...I don't know...work...travel...'

'Oh,' she whimpered. Then she quietly went back to the kitchen. That's it? I thought. That was all she was going to say? My mom was being surprisingly docile about this. And here I had expected full-blown psychological warfare. I was just beginning to breathe evenly when it hit me.

My mom wasn't being docile. She was merely stalling. She was merely being proverbially calm before her trademark storm.

My worst suspicion was confirmed when, in a few seconds, she filed out of the kitchen, rolling pin in one hand and Heavily-buttered Paratha No. 6 in the other. She smacked the paratha on to my plate, ground her heels into the carpet, flared her nostrils and EX—PLO—DED... into (what Dad and I call), MOM'S SIGNATURE RANT...

For the next twenty minutes, (in keeping with the norm) I was dragged across a long guilt trip. Questions of the 'Have-I-been-a-bad-mother' variety were dramatically speared at me with an expectation of the obligatory denial. Unfortunately, when the obligatory denial didn't come forth (since it had gotten stuck in my throat along with the first bite of Heavily-buttered Paratha No. 6), Bollywood-style tear-jerks followed.

Mid-way through the whole tear-stained drama, I had a déjà vu moment—a memory flash from a few years ago, when my mom had caught me choking on my first and last Wills Ultra Mild in the corner of my balcony. 'Is this what you do behind our backs?' my mom had chided. 'Are these the kind of values we have taught you? What will people think? What sort of a girl smokes...' The tirade had lasted for a whole hour.

I tuned into the present and looked at my watch. Judging from past trends, my mom had another twenty-seven minutes of her dirge to go through. She had moved on from 'Have I been a bad mother?' to 'This is what happens when you get too much freedom'. I hadn't missed much. I stifled a yawn, tuned out again, and began worrying about how many sit-ups I would have to do to get rid of all the butter that had settled on my hips. When I eventually came around to the present, twenty-five minutes later, it was to the words: 'Nothing doing. You are meeting that nice boy.'

Bugger. After rambling all over town we were back to square one? It was clearly time to INTERVENE.

'But mom,' I began, getting up from my chair. Too late. She had already flung her rolling pin down and marched out of the room. I slowly sat down and began rubbing my throbbing forehead.

'So you are joining work on Monday?' my dad asked, out of the blue. I started. I had forgotten that he was still in the room. I turned to him in a daze. 'Yes,' I said flatly. He nodded. 'Will you be staying with your aunt?' he asked.

'Only for a few days. Then I'll find a place on rent.'

He nodded again. Then he went back to reading his newspaper, leaving me to my woes. Twenty-five years of being married to my mom had made him a very strong advocate of the ostrich school of thought. I didn't blame him.

I reached the Head Office dot at 8.30 a.m. on Monday morning. I had barely signed the muster when I received a call from Glasses-n-Whiskers from HR. 'You will be reporting to The Sales Head directly,' she said. 'Go to the second floor. He is expecting you this minute in his cabin.' My heart sank all the way to my big feet. *Directly report* to Wimp-eater? *Why God why?* And here I had been hoping to report to someone lower down the rung—a buffer between Wimp-eater and me. Just my rotten luck that I was now going to be in the direct line of firing instead, completely buffer-less. I stepped out of my cubicle and slowly walked towards his cabin, panic balling up in my chest. It seemed to me that I had been hoisted from the frying pan of Chhota Don only to get flung into the fire of Wimp-eater.

When I entered Wimp-eater's cabin a moment later, he was pacing behind his desk, animatedly talking into his phone. He signalled me to take a seat. I sat down without a sound and nervously chewed my lip. A few minutes later, Wimp-eater plonked down on his chair with a heavy thud. 'These branch managers,' he groused, running an agitated hand through his hair, 'bunch of idiots, I tell you.' I cringed and smiled awkwardly. Wimp-eater leaned back in his chair and looked at me for a long moment.

'The reason we decided to bring you to the Head Office,' he eventually said, resting his forearms on the table, 'is because you did well on the market mapping project...'

I blinked. *Eh? Did what?*

'...Your boss in Delhi said you did a really good job...'

Um, he said what now?

'...I have to say he was really impressed.'

Excuse me? You talkin' to me? I rotated around just to be sure. Nope. No one there. Just me.

I rotated back to Wimp-eater. He seemed to be waiting for me to respond. I simply stared, bug-eyed and mute. *I had done a good job? I? Me? Moi? Had Chhota Don really said that? When? Why? How? Wait a minute...I* yanked up...*Had I just landed in some parallel universe? A universe in which Mr Darcy existed, and he and I shacked up?*

It appeared, rather fortunately, that I had indeed landed in such a parallel universe, because Wimp-eater was almost smiling now and saying, 'You have mapped close to 900 outlets, your boss told me. That is very good.'

I lifted my dropped jaw. 'Er, thank you, Sir,' I managed to squeak. Suddenly, a tiny doubt flitted insidiously into my head. Had Chhota Don praised me to Wimp-eater so that he could have me shipped off to Mumbai? I brooded on that thought for a moment, then decided that even if that were the case, I didn't care. For the first time since I had joined J&K, I was being regarded as a person with IQ. I was damned if I wasn't going to be happy about it. 'Thank you Sir,' I said again, this time with a big smile. Wimp-eater nodded, then opened an excel sheet on his laptop. 'Your new role,' he said gruffly, 'is MIS Sales.' He paused for a moment, then elaborated, 'that means, you will be managing the information system for sales.'

Aha, MIS Sales, I thought with glee—The Schmoozer's secret project. This must be terribly important. I beamed like an eager child and leaned forward. Eagerness quickly turned to dismay, as I gleaned from Wimp-eater's next few words that MIS Sales was just a code for hounding all the branches for their market mapping reports and collating them in colourful excel sheets. *Will I never get rid of market mapping?* I inwardly moaned. Then I remembered Lara who was still out there spinning around in some market and realized that I was better off. No wait, I was better than just 'better off'. Wimp-eater had practically conferred upon me the title of Star Trainee With Bright Future. It couldn't get better than that.

I decided right then that I would not let him down. From now on I would be a model of brilliance and efficiency, so that a year from now, Wimp-eater would have no choice but to promote me to Manager. My impending rise to greatness instantly perked me up. Soon, I would devise brilliant marketing strategies that would make J&K a force to be reckoned with. I would be desperately sought after by top Marketing companies of the world, but out of loyalty to J&K, I would refuse them all. For my loyalty, I would be duly rewarded with a penthouse flat and a Mercedes Benz, of course.

By the time I left Wimp-eater's office, in my mind I was already CEO of J&K. Nose in the air, I almost danced over to my cubicle, whistling.

For the rest of the week, I concentrated all my efforts on flat-hunting, eventually closing in on a tiny, yet airy 2-BHK apartment about fifty minutes from my office. Predictably, the rent was rather steep, but I was determined to immediately remedy the situation by hunting for a room-mate. 'Are you sure you want to move out?' my aunt asked one night, during a two-minute commercial break of CID. 'Yes,' I told her, 'I'm quite hooked to being independent.' It was, perhaps, the only bit about my stay in Delhi that I had enjoyed. My aunt seemed to understand, for she nodded a couple of times, before returning her attention to the TV.

The following weekend, deposit paid, I moved into my flat with luggage and Coolio. I felt like a new and improved person. New role. New flat. New confidence. Hell, even Coolio had donned a New Avatar, having traded its 'Starved Somalian-Victim' look for 'Healthy Happy Fat-cat' Look (courtesy its new and improved owner).

In the following days, I slipped into a pattern: swiping my card by 8.30 a.m., settling into my cubicle with a cup of coffee, calling up branches for various reports, and then happily twiddling my thumbs till they arrived later in the day. Then, after collating those reports (which took all of 85 minutes) and happily twiddling my thumbs, again, till 5.30 p.m., I would, at that point, nab my bag and merrily bolt from the premises.

Mercifully, I did not have to interact much with Wimp-eater, who for the most part, remained holed up in his cabin with his right hand man—a short, thin, nervous looking chap who always looked like he was into something terribly important. Right Hand Man was Wimp-eater's personal assistant. When Wimp-eater boomed, 'Jump!' Right Hand Man jumped. And when Wimp-eater wanted to bitch about his boss (The CEO), Right Hand Man served as his dutiful venting board.

That The CEO was deeply feared was something that became increasingly evident to me. And not just by the Wimp-eater, but also by all employees on the Sales and Marketing floor. 'He can be really nasty,' I heard one of the Marketing girls grouse to her colleague one day in the washroom before she caught sight of me and hushed up. I was rather bewildered. My own memory of The CEO was centred on the image of a rather benign looking man sitting next to Glasses-n-Moustache, during my interview, and staring at his shoe. Could that harmless looking man really be that bad? The answer came knocking at my door, all too soon.

It was 5.29 p.m. on a Friday evening, and after having spent the whole day blankly staring at an excel sheet and chain-sipping coffees, I was all set to leave for the day. I switched off my laptop, packed it into my bag and at precisely 5.30 p.m., was halfway past my cubicle, when The CEO stepped out of his cabin and spotted me. He looked at his watch pointedly and frowned. I froze on the spot, my happy little smile buckling.

'Leaving already?' he drawled. 'Er, yes Sir,' I managed, breathless. 'Did you leave at this hour even at the branch office?' he questioned, his eyes narrowed.

'Er, no Sir,' I mumbled. There was a pause. Feeling an overwhelming need to fill it, I blabbed, 'Things were more hectic there, Sir.'

The CEO's eyebrows shot up. 'I see,' he said slowly. Then he turned and walked away. I eased my shoulders in relief, then waited till he was out of sight before catapulting out like a bullet.

By the time I reached home, I had dismissed the entire scene from my mind. But the next morning, as soon as I walked in, The CEO's secretary scuttled towards me, Bad News written all over her wrinkly face. 'The CEO wants to see you in his cabin,' she whispered ominously.

My heart sank a little. I kept my bag on my table, walked towards his cabin and knocked on the door. What on earth could he want, I brooded.

'Come in,' he yelled. Feeling weak-kneed, I brushed a loose strand of hair out of my eyes and entered his cabin. The CEO was not alone. Across the table, facing him, sat Wimp-eater, who was watching me with a questioning look. I crept forward and stealthily drew up a chair next to him. I was beginning to feel rather terrified.

'So,' The CEO began slowly, almost casually, when I was seated. He was looking at Wimp-eater. 'Do you know what this girl was saying yesterday?' Wimp-eater shook his head. My forehead creased in a frown. *What had I said yesterday?* 'She was saying that you don't keep her busy enough. That you are not giving her any work. That you are keeping her idle. Now why is that?'

Eh? What? I mentally sputtered, gripping the arms of my chair. *When the hell had I said that?* I turned wildly to Wimp-eater. His jaw looked a little knotty.

'No need to look at him,' The CEO drawled. My head swung back to him. A sly smile was now playing on his lips. 'It's your boss's job to keep you busy,' he said, 'and clearly he isn't doing that.' I sat up in my chair and blinked at him, my mouth a perfect 'O'. The realization that he was far from harmless, had finally sliced through me. Wimp-eater didn't say a word. I was itching to look at his face, but I dared not.

The CEO had now moved on and was asking Wimp-eater about some sales report. Wimp-eater answered briefly. The CEO nodded, then turning to his laptop, dismissed us with a flick of his hand.

Wimp-eater left first. I guiltily hotfooted after him.

'Sir,' I began shakily, as he marched towards his cabin. He turned to me, his face set in fury. 'S-sir,' I stammered, gazing beseechingly at him, 'I didn't really say that…I mean, what I had said was…'

'I don't care,' Wimp-eater growled through clenched teeth. An angry vein was pulsating on his forehead. Any second now, I thought it would burst. 'Unlike some people, I have work to do,' he stated pointedly, then strode into his cabin, swinging the door shut in my face. I turned around glumly and drooped into my chair.

Feeling light-headed with panic, I took a few deep breaths to calm myself down. Unfortunately, calm didn't come, only a voice telling me that I had just moved from being Star Trainee With Bright Future to being Stupid Trainee With No Future. Eyes filled with miserable tears, I clicked open a new email page in Microsoft Outlook and began punching my keyboard.

Memo: To: The CEO, (I typed)

1. Did you have to spot me charging out of office at 5.30 p.m. yesterday?

2. Did you have to automatically assume that bolting at 5.30= being jobless (which, FYI, I am not. Ok, maybe I am, a little. But 5.30 p.m. is the official closure time.)

3. Did you have to, the next day, sneakily kill two birds with one stone?
   - Bird No.1: Good ol' me
   - Bird No. 2: Wimp-eater (whom you hate because he is eyeing your post)

   Stone: Telling Wimp-eater that it is his fault that I am jobless.

4. Did you have to sit back and smirk, while a rabid Wimp-eater refused to even look at me?

5. Most of all, did you have to burst my 'Coming-to-Mumbai'
    sunshine bubble?

And to think that I thought that you were a harmless old man,
albeit with hair in a grave stage of comb-over. More fool me.

I read the memo three times, then pressed delete.

In the following week, three things happened. A) Wimp-
eater began to ignore me (a situation I was already all too
familiar with), choosing to communicate with me only via
Right Hand Man; B) Right Hand Man, on Wimp-eater's orders,
began dumping me with all sorts of bunkum data-entry work;
and C) The CEO began to provide me with more and more
glimpses of his Nasty Side.

One such glimpse was flashed during the monthly Sales and
Marketing meeting, which Wimp-eater (through his Right Hand
Man) had ordered me to attend. Our sales figures were dipping
and Wimp-eater as well as the Marketing Head had planned to
present their strategies to The CEO to tackle the same. Half
way through the Marketing Head's presentation, The CEO
cracked his fist on the table. 'That's enough!' he stormed,
holding up his hand. 'This is all humbug…nothing but a whole
lot of intellectual masturbation…You characters are just a bunch
of incompetent morons wasting my time…!'

I sat still for a moment, completely stunned, then slowly
peeped into The Marketing Head's face. He looked
expressionless. So did the Wimp-eater, who was leaning back in
a chair next to him, tapping a pencil on the table. I scanned the
rest of the faces in the room. Expressionless, each one of them,
as if carved out of the local granite. Either they were all genuinely
unaffected by The CEO's verbal lashing, I thought, or, I was
surrounded by a bunch of people who subscribed to the John
Abraham School of acting.

After that meeting, I became terminally terrified of The CEO. His cabin faced my cubicle and every time the door opened, my heart would leap into my mouth and my stomach would cramp up viciously. I began to wonder whether I'd been better off in Delhi. At least, there, I was left to my own devices, well out of range of Chhota Don's honking big nose. Memories of me traipsing around in the Delhi markets flooded my mind; memories that I now viewed through the pretty, rose-tinted glasses of nostalgia. 'Ah, those happy days,' I lamented one evening.

It was 8.15 p.m. and The CEO had just thrown me a sadistic 'hah-not-quite-so-free-these-days-are-you?' look, before striding into his cabin. I slid further down in my chair and rubbed my bloodshot eyes. I had been doing ten-hours-per-day of non-stop data entry work for the last week. And it was all thanks to that man. Suddenly I found myself missing Chhota Don, even ASMs 1 to 4. I felt an almost overwhelming urge to run out of the office, board a flight to Delhi, kiss Chhota Don's feet and beg him to take me back.

My phone buzzed on my table. I flicked a weary glance at it.
Lara: HOWZ D WORK LIFE WITH D WIMP-EATER? AND D LOVE LIFE WITH D VELCRO MAN?
I texted back.
BOTH ARE D SCUM
Yes, things with Velcro Man had not shown any improvement either. While I had been working non-stop, Velcro Man—in vintage Velcro Man fashion—had been calling me up daily and whining *non-stop*.

Monday
(*Non-stop* from 8.10 to 8.50 p.m.): Velcro man whines about The Potholes in Bangalore.

Me: (to myself) I must dump him. I must dump him. I must dump him.

Tuesday
(*Non-stop* from 7.06 to 7.43 p.m.): Velcro man whines about Rising Price of Fuel.
Me: (to myself) I must dump him. I must dump him. I must dump him.

Wednesday
(*Non-stop* from 9.16 to 9.50 p.m.): Velcro man whines about Downturn in Indian Cricket.
Me: (to myself) I must dump him etc. etc.

Thursday
(*Non-stop* from 6.45 to 7.13 p.m.): Velcro man whines about World Economy and Global Financial Crisis.
Me: (to myself) I must dump him etc. etc.

Friday
(*Non-stop* from 10.03 to 10.37 p.m.): Velcro man whines about Hole in the Ozone Layer.
Me: (to myself) I must etc. etc.

Except that it was now Friday evening of the *following* week and I still hadn't dumped him. I couldn't help it. Wimp-eater was still giving me the cold shoulder. Right Hand Man was still dumping me with data entry work. And The CEO was still monitoring my every move and revelling in my misery. Consequently, I was feeling needy and clingy and in no mood for a break up. Unfortunately, this could mean only one thing...

...I was practically Velcro Woman.

9

Two days later, on Sunday evening, I was firmly in the Bell Jar.
Not only was I staring at the fact that I was needy-clingy-Velcro-
Woman, but also at the knowledge that the next day was a
dratted Monday. I had never felt so blue in my life. I lay in my
bed — my residence for the past five hours — bunched under a
duvet, digging into a tub of ice cream between arbitrary channel-
flips from my remote. A half-hour and a near-empty tub later, I
was vacantly staring at some has-been actor peddling a tonic for
Rejuvenated Sex Life on some teleshopping network, when my
room-mate waltzed into my room. (Yes, I now had a room-
mate). FYI, she was:

- 24 years old
- Product Manager of some fancy-schmancy make-up brand
  and
- On a mission to paint the face of the World and Its
  Mother with her brand's over-priced products.

Oh and she was also, by habit, disgustingly perky on Sunday
evenings.

'Moping already?' she asked, viewing first my untidy room,
then me; and then wrinkling her nose at both.

'Mmm,' I mumbled, mouth full of ice-cream.

'But it's just 5 p.m. The weekend is still young!'

I glanced at her over the rim of my tub. 'The weekend died
at 12 p.m. this afternoon and I am in mourning.'

'Wow. You must really hate your job.'

'Well, duh,' I grunted, turning back to my tub.

'But why?' she asked dimly.

God. The woman was like a badger. 'Don't you have some fancy fashion thing to go to?' I niggled, wriggling further down my bed.

'*Yes*' she squealed. 'It's the Fashion Week. All the top designers are going to be there! I've got an extra pass! Want to come?'

I shook my head. 'Sorry, but I'm just going to watch Mr Idiot Box here and wallow in my drivel'

An appalled intake of breath followed. I could see a thought bubble floating over her chemically-curled hair. It hurled: *Loser!*

I defiantly took another dig at my ice-cream, then *OUCH!* as the nerves in my teeth revolted.

'You know, if you hate your job so much, you should just look for another one,' she said, before strutting out on her three-inch stilettos.

YOUR FRIEND IS REALLY ANNOYING, I made haste to text Lara. Chemical Curls had been rewarded with the post of My Room-mate, after a glowing recommendation from Lara whom she had been 'best-pals' with in college. 'She is a complete hoot,' Lara had told me. So far, with her squeaky stilettos, her exclamation-mark infested sentences and her boundless love for her job, she was more of a pain and less of a hoot.

AWW GIVE HER SOME TIME, YOU. SHE IS A SWEETHEART.

I snorted and went back to my tub.

In the following weeks, things at work began to get more and more chaotic. The fridge division was in trouble. Sales were dipping even further and The CEO and Wimp-eater were spitting fire in all directions. The entire floor was like a war zone, with everybody wondering who would be next in line to get blown to bits. Rumours that, as a last ditch effort towards reviving the division, The CEO had employed the services of a global consulting firm, were beginning to do the rounds. Like the other employees, I began to wonder if that meant that heads would start rolling. The thought did nothing for my peace of mind; something told me that if The CEO or Wimp-eater made a list of 'Heads That Ought To Roll', my name would feature at the top.

One morning, while I was on a phone-call with one of the branch managers, Wimp-eater stuck his head out of his cabin and called me in. I walked over, and was just about to take a seat when I noticed a youngish man, leaning against the wall by the window. I nearly did a double take as I saw his face. He was cuuute. A bit smug-looking, but cuute. And ooooh, he was tall too! At least 6 feet, 2 inches. I sat down in my chair and jiggled my foot to stop myself from ogling. Who was he? I wondered. He couldn't be from J&K. I mean, J&K's men were primarily a bunch of old uncles.

Pretty Boy, I soon learnt, was a Top consultant from a Top consultancy firm, sent on a mission to rescue J&K's dying brands. 'He will be stationed in our office for the next few months,' Wimp-eater explained. He had been speaking of Pretty Boy in glowing hyperbole…'And he'll be working on a project to help expand our distribution network and increase our sales.' Wimp-eater paused for a second, in the middle of what had seemed to be an anthem without end, and added, 'In the next few weeks, he will need sales data from you, and you will be expected to extend your full cooperation in this regard.' I nodded quickly, then discretely skimmed over Pretty Boy's face again. He was staring at his shoe, lost in thought. I fought off a swoon; he really did look pretty.

But as the days wore on, my initial excitement over Pretty Boy's prettiness began to fade; because it turned out that Pretty Boy came with special abilities: 1) Creating colourful excel formats and 2) Hounding me black-n-blue till I populated said colourful excel formats with blah data. Who would have known? Every time I looked up from my laptop, there he was, walking towards me, looking all important, wanting some damn data or the other and being thoroughly arrogant about it.

Much like right now.

'I want the distribution data for the Kerala branch. You haven't filled that into the format I sent you.' Pretty Boy was towering over my desk, arms crossed, impatient.

'Which format?' I asked, voice dripping with sarcasm. 'You've sent so many.'

His eyes narrowed. 'The one that I sent you this morning.'

'Fine,' I grouched, 'I'll send it.'

'When?'

'Tomorrow.'

'I want it today,' he said, then without waiting for me to reply, turned on his heel and stalked off. I sent daggers at his retreating back. Arrogant peace of junk. Just because he drew a salary the size of the National Debt of Angola, didn't mean that he had to carry around an ego the size of China. I was speedily tiring of extending my 'full cooperation' to him, especially when what I really wanted to extend to him, was my fist, all the way up to his face.

And ok, alright, it was a pretty face. But so what? He seemed quite besotted with Shiny-Faced-Trainee No. 1 from Marketing, whom he wasted no chance flirting with when he wasn't playing 'data scavenger'. My eyes quickly darted to the water cooler, where Shiny-Faced-Trainee No. 1, at that moment, stood batting her eyelids at Pretty Boy like Mata Hari.

I closed my eyes and tried to not throw-up over them. Why should I care if he was flirting with Shiny-Faced-Trainee No. 1? I had a boyfriend already. I was seeing Velcro Man.

Oh God, *why* was I still seeing Velcro Man?

I shook my head and turned back to the screen. Pretty Boy's 52nd colourful excel format stared back at me. I was just about to resume populating it when Wimp-eater's cabin door flew open. My eyes darted to him as he stepped out and marched towards me. 'I want the network reach and share figures for North—Rural,' he barked. I froze, my mind going blank with terror.

'Quick, I don't have all day.'

I looked at my laptop screen and blinked. *North—Rural. Which folder had I kept that file in?*

'Quick, quick, quick, the CEO needs it *now*,' Wimp-eater sailed into me. I felt unhinged. The man was looming over me like a helicopter. I could barely focus. Shaking inwardly, I tried to think. *Did I keep it in the folder called Updated Figures?* I clicked on it. Not there. My heart sank.

'Don't you have it?' Wimp-eater asked irascibly. 'I have it S-sir,' I faltered, not daring to look up. I clicked on another folder. Not there either. Wimp-eater was now clucking impatiently. 'Come on, out with it. I'm ageing here,' he roared. Everyone on the floor was now looking at me. From the corner of my eye, I could see Right Hand Man shaking his head. I felt my cheeks flame. God, this was mortifying beyond my worst nightmares. All I wanted to do was to wither away and cease existing. I clicked on two more folders. The file was not in either one of them. *Where the hell have I kept that damn file?*

'If you can't give me the data I need,' Wimp-eater was now blasting my eardrums, 'then what the hell am I paying you for, you...you good-for-nothing trainee!!' Then he about-turned, stormed off into his cabin and slammed the door shut. I shrivelled up in my chair, my heart hammering. A familiar heat burned around my eyes. I am not going to cry, I told myself. *I am NOT going to cry. Not when everyone is still looking at me. Not when Pretty Boy and Shiny-Faced-Trainee No. 1 are bugging their eyes out at me.* I bit my tongue to suppress a threatening flood of tears. *I'm not going to cry. NOT going to cry.* A tear slipped down my cheek. I defiantly brushed it off. I took a deep, shuddering breath and resumed trying to locate the file. After a bit, I e-mailed it to Wimp-eater.

Feeling the onset of another outbreak of tears, I was about to head to the washroom, when the shadow of Pretty Boy's pretty head appeared over my screen.

I sniffed and looked up. 'Look,' I began, 'whatever data you need...'

'I don't need data,' Pretty Boy broke in, 'just thought, I'd ask if you were...' he stopped, then started again...'if you were alright?'

'Of course,' I said, with affected nonchalance and stared at a spot on my screen. Huge, fat tears were filming my eyes. I fought off a sniffle and nearly choked.

A second later, I darted a quick peek at Pretty Boy. He was looking at me as if he could see everything that was going on in my head. 'It's not *you*, you know, it's *him*' he said gently. 'The man has been biting everyone's head off.'

I turned to my screen, defiant and still. I didn't need anyone's pity. Especially not Pretty Boy's. He could take his pity and stuff it...

Pretty Boy remained for a long moment near my cubicle as if he wanted to say something more, then unobtrusivelyly turned and walked back to Shiny-Faced-Trainee No. 1's cubicle. I could see him whisper something to her. Shiny-Faced-Trainee No. 1 quickly glanced at me, then back at Pretty Boy. I curled my hands into fists under my desk. So they were talking about me, probably making fun of me too. Well, fine. Whatever. I didn't care.

I had more important things to do, such as typing my resignation letter. After all, enough was enough. What did Wimp-eater think I was? Some data vending machine with instructions reading: 'Insert peanuts. Yelp out order. Wait for machine to whoosh out data at speed of light?' In the last few months, I had been lashed left right and centre. I had had lashing up to my eyeballs. No more. It stopped here. I was putting in my papers and Wimp-eater, The CEO, Pretty Boy, well, the whole lot of them could simply fall into hell. I uncurled my hands and began typing.

<u>Resignation Letter (Draft 1):</u>

Dear Boss,
I regret to inform you that I am resigning as Management Trainee, effective two weeks from today. I thank you for the opportunity to work here. My stint in this Company has provided me with a truly rich and valuable experience.

Wishing you all the very best,
Yours sincerely,
Zoey Verma

<u>Resignation Letter (Draft 2):</u>

Dear Boss,

It gives me a whooping thrill to inform you that I am resigning as Management Trainee, effective immediately. I thank you for successfully sucking the joy out of my life. My stint in this Company has provided me with a truly rich experience—that of recurring migraines, raging ulcers and a roof-hitting Blood Pressure.

Wishing you all the very best in figuring out where all my files are—May you have better luck at it than I did.

Also wishing you the very best in handling Pretty Boy. May he prove to be as concentrated a pain in your backside, as he has been in mine.

Yours sincerely,
An Ecstatic Ex-employee

<u>Resignation Letter (Draft 3):</u>

You big jerk. I quit.

I didn't put in my papers that day. Good sense kicked in just as I was about to walk into Wimp-eater's cabin with a printout of Resignation Letter Draft 3, and advised that it would be wiser to sleep over my decision. *It is Friday evening. Wait till Monday morning, before taking the plunge,* it cautioned.

On my way home, that evening, I decided to apprise Lara of recent events. *Nearly got fired,* I texted, then sat back and waited for her to send me a few words of comfort.

They came exactly five seconds later.

Hang in there, u mite get lucky the next time..

Despite Lara's 'words of comfort', my mortification over the afternoon's experience echoed throughout the rest of the evening. I kept recalling Wimp-eater's words and cringing inwardly. Finally, unable to bear it any longer, I decided to call up Velcro Man that night to sob on his long-distance shoulder. This time I wasn't going to let *him* whine. This time *I* was going to do all the whining, because I had nearly been fired and there was no way Velcro Man could top that. I rubbed my hands with grit as I dialled Velcro Man's number. Operation Whine-a-Lot here I come.

Later that night...

Me (all charged up): 'Hi.'

Velcro Man: 'Hey...'

Me (before he can get another word in): 'You won't believe what happened today...'

Velcro Man: 'Yeah, God, I had such a day, you won't believe it. My mo...'

Me (cutting him short): 'Yes, yes...but I had a really bad day today...'

Velcro Man: 'Really? God...so did I...worse I think...My mo...'

Me (determined not to get side-tracked): 'I'm quite sure my day was worse...way worse than yours...'

Velcro Man: 'Really? Well I don't know about that because you see, my m...'

Me (beginning to get a bit hysterical): 'I WAS NEARLY FIRED!'

Velcro Man: 'Nearly? So you weren't fired?'

Me (faltering): 'Erm, no, but...'

Velcro Man: 'That's good then...'

Me (recovering): 'No, it's not, it's not good...'

Velcro Man: 'Why? Did you want to get fired?'

Me (confused): 'What? No, no, of course not...'

Velcro Man: 'Then like I said, it's all good. Now as I was saying, my mo...'

Me (completely hysterical now): 'Excuse me? Don't you get it? I had a really bad day...REALLY BAD...it was terrible...TERRIBLE...Wimp-eater wanted some data...he kept yelling...I couldn't think straight...everyone kept looking...'

Velcro Man: 'My mom had an accident...'

Me (words continuing to tumble forth): '...that bitch from marketing...Shiny-Faced-Trainee...kept gaping at me...was smirking behind her hand...God, I hate her...always so shiny...always asking questions...and batting her eyelids...pouting and flirting...who does she think she is...wait...*what*...*what did you say?*'

Velcro Man: 'Mom had an accident. She has been hospitalized.'

Me (speechless): 'Oh...'

Turned out, it wasn't a major accident. A fall in the bathroom: a few minor bruises and a sprained ankle. But Velcro Man was inconsolable. And I couldn't be a heartless bitch. And so, I ended up abandoning Operation Whine-a-Lot and spending the next age, *once again* listening to Velcro Man slobber all over *my* long distance shoulder.

'You are probably stuck in the wrong career,' Chemical Curls said, as my butter fingers dropped my flat-pick for the nth time.

It was Saturday morning. Chemical Curls and I were sitting in the verandah of a charming little Goan-style house, guitars straddling our laps. It had been a month since Chemical Curls had forced me to sign up for guitar lessons. In the course of the four lessons that we had had since, I had acquired four bruised finger tips and the knowledge that I had no talent, whatsoever, for playing the instrument. Thanks to that, and the previous day's events, I had been in no mood to go strumming that morning. I had told Chemical Curls as much, but she had had none of it and had practically frogmarched me to the class. Now, instead of following through with the lesson, she had taken it upon herself to 'career counsel' me.

'Seriously, have you thought about it? A career change, that is?'

'What am I supposed to do? Become a rockstar?' I mumbled, picking up the flat-pick.

A grunt escaped from Octus, our guitar instructor, who had been trying to get us to tune our guitars for what seemed like ages now.

'Oh come on,' Chemical Curls said, cradling her guitar as if it were a baby. 'There must be something you are good at?'

'Guys, that is not how you hold a guitar…' Octus yowled.

'No,' I snapped, prodding my guitar with my fist. 'I am congenitally talentless.'

'Guys, you'll need to strum your guitars, not beat them,' said Octus, aghast.

'Really, Zoey? Are you telling me that there's nothing you are good at?' Chemical Curls scorned. 'I don't believe it.'

'It's true,' I lamented.

'Guys, you'll need to focus, man,' Octus cribbed. 'This ain't a candle making class man…'

Chemical Curls ignored Octus. 'You need to just sit down and think about what you really want to do Zoey…what makes you happy.'

'I don't know,' I said, ignoring Octus too. 'I mean, if my calling in life hasn't come-a-calling in the last twenty-three years, what are the chances it will come to me now?'

'None,' Octus huffed, looking just about ready to thwack us both with his guitar. Poor Octus. He was stuck with teaching a pair of hopeless, strumming-challenged girls, when he'd rather have been out there following Slash's footsteps.

That morning, a couple of hours after the guitar class, I packed an overnight bag and boarded a bus to Pune. I hadn't been to visit my folks since the drama of the last trip and, quite frankly, I had hoped to avoid another face-to-face meeting with my mom for the next forty aeons at the very least. But unfortunately, due to unavoidable circumstances, the face-to-face meeting was now going to happen sooner than planned. The unavoidable circumstance, as it turned out, was Sabina aunty. She had come down to visit my folks after almost six months and had insisted on meeting me as well. I wasn't looking forward to this meeting—I could smell melodrama all the way from the bus.

The maid opened the door when I pressed the bell three hours later. I walked into the hall to the sight of my dad watering the plants in the balcony and my mom and Sabina aunty sitting at the centre table with a plate heaped (and I mean, *heaped*) with colossal laddoos. 'Zoey!' Aunty exclaimed when she saw me. She got up, hugged me within an inch of my life, then dragged me to the sofa. I smiled weakly and sat down; then flitted a look at my mom, who clawed her eyes into mine before swinging her nose to the ceiling. Great. She was clearly still angry with me.

'How are you, beta? You look so pale,' Aunty cooed, pulling my cheeks.

'I'm fine Aunty,' I murmured. 'How is Mira?' Mira was her daughter (the same one who was six months younger than me and getting married to some random dude 'from the internet').

'She is fine. She is getting married. She is great,' chanted Aunty. 'He is such a good boy. We found him on the internet…He is so good…Earning so well…'

'Great,' I said. Mom harrumphed.

'And what about you beta, how is work going?' she asked.

'It's going on,' I said evasively.

'And have you started looking for a boy for her?' Aunty turned to my mom.

'What looking?' my mom yapped. 'Tell aunty,' she said, glaring at me, 'tell her about your plans.'

'What plans?' Aunty asked, intrigued.

'Er, nothing,' I said with annoyance. 'Just that I have no intention of marrying at least for the next three years.'

'Hain? Kyon?' Aunty wheezed, her eyeballs widening into perfect orbs. Then twisting her neck to face my mom, she accosted her with, 'Nisha? Are you not looking for a boy for her?'

My mom flared her nostrils pointedly.

'Marriage is the last thing on my mind,' I broke in before she could say anything.

'Why? What else is there on your mind?' Aunty asked dimly, picking up a laddoo.

'Er,' I faltered, 'many things. For starters, I've decided…' (I decided this as I spoke)…'to do some travelling. I'm going to quit my job soon to travel for some months.'

My mom's head swivelled around in shock. That it didn't fall off is a wonder.

'What? Quit your job? To travel? Have you gone mad?' She was now flapping her arms wildly. 'You just got a job. Why do you want to leave it? Do you think jobs grow on trees? Like good boys?'

'I want to see the world,' I declared brightly. That sounded lame even to my own ears.

There was an alarmed pause, before my aunt croaked, 'But what is there to see? A mountain in London is no different from a mountain in Lonavala. A tree in New York is the same as…as…'

'A tree in Navi Mumbai,' my mom supplied with satisfaction.

'Actually, that is not entirely true,' chipped in my dad placidly, who had till this point still been watering the plants. My mom winged him a fierce look and sniped, 'What do you know?' Then she looked at me, attacking, 'Of course Aunty is right.'

Poor dad. He didn't stand a chance. He went back to watering the plants.

'Beta, first get married,' said Aunty, 'then do all this break-shake. At least then your husband can support you.'

'I don't need to be supported,' I spat out, my head crackling with rage. 'I have savings.' (I didn't. Not yet anyway. But that was beside the point).

'Oof…kids these days,' she tutted, turning to my mom, 'they only want to spend. They think money grows on trees.'

I looked at my Mom and aunt, as they exchanged expressions of dismay and shook their heads in unison. Two melodramatic peas in a pod. Frankly I was speedily tiring of all the drama…I had had ENOUGH. That's it. NO MORE. I was done. I picked up my overnight bag and stormed out of the hall.

'Where are you going?' I heard Aunty exclaim. 'You haven't eaten any laddoos…'

'Not hungry,' I growled.

'I hope you have put up her profile on the matrimonial sites,' were the last words I heard before I flung the door of my bedroom shut.

Profile on a matrimonial site, huh? Sure, I could think of one to go on it:

> Clueless and soon-to-be jobless female with big feet and hair
> like Medusa seeks male with healthy appreciation for psycho
> in laws and high-pitched melodrama. Bonus points for 'Saas
> Bahu' serial addicts.

I was still fuming ninety minutes later, when I heard a knock on my door. Opening it, I saw it was my dad. He was poised outside tentatively, a watering can in one hand and his specs in the other.

'Are you alright?' he asked.

'Yeah,' I nodded sadly.

'Are you really thinking about quitting your job?' he asked, running thin, knotty fingers through his fast disappearing hair.

I sighed, turned and flopped back on my bed. 'Yes.'

Dad entered the room and looked around. He appeared lost, as if he were a pet poodle that had suddenly found itself let loose at a peak-hour traffic signal in Mumbai.

'Why?' he asked, donning his glasses and blinking at me from behind them.

'Why what?'

'Why do you want to quit?'

'I told you why. To travel,' I said defiantly.

He squeezed the bridge of his nose. 'Is that the real reason?'

A pause followed. I studied my fingernails. 'I don't know,' I finally said, 'I think I suck at what I do anyway…'

He said nothing for a few seconds.

'And my boss thinks I should quit,' I added miserably.

'Do *you* think you should quit?' he asked, his voice light.

'I don't know…' I stopped, unsure.

'You know,' he said, clearing his throat, 'you've always underestimated yourself.'

'Have I?' I asked, quickly looking up at my dad, then away again.

'Yes,' he said, nodding reflectively. 'It's what you are doing now.'

'No,' I protested, 'I told you that my boss thinks I'm no good.'

'So?' Dad asked.

'So, I'm beginning to think he's right,' I said flatly.

'Perhaps that is the problem,' he said kindly, then he came forward, patted my back affectionately, and soundlessly walked out.

I crossed my arms and stared at the spot in my room where he had stood. Damn my dad and his genius logic.

10

I didn't put in my papers on the following Monday either. I told myself that quitting my first job within six months would not look good on my CV. But I suspect that the real reason was that I did not want to call it quits on a bad note. If nothing else, I wanted to reclaim a sliver of dignity (even though chances of that happening seemed slim; non-existent, in fact.)

Days crawled into weeks and eventually, I found myself up close to the month of February. I had now spent exactly 8 months, 1 week and 3 days in the employ of J&K. (Yes, I was counting down, although I wasn't quite sure to what.)

On a Wednesday morning, in the first week of the month, we were all summoned to the conference room for the monthly Sales and Marketing meeting. Now, usually these meetings were a big yawn (big surprise), but this particular one promised to be different. It was, after all, the meeting where we would see Pretty Boy present for the first time. Having spent almost two months ruminating over my duly filled excel formats, Pretty Boy was now all set to justify his existence by presenting an interim report on 'How to Optimise the Fridge Sales Network of J&K'. The Top Bosses were eager. They couldn't wait. All-Knowing Pretty Boy was soon going to whip out the key to all their problems.

They were already present in the room when Pretty Boy

arrived (making a grand late entry). He loped in, his head bobbing, almost as if he could hear the sound of a drum-roll in it. Then he stood at the head of the oval table, surveying his audience, sunbathing in the warmth of their attention. 'Good morning,' he boomed. 'Good morning,' everyone chimed. 'Let's get this show started!' He leaned forward to click open his first slide. What followed next had everyone in a trance. Bar diagrams swooped in, sales figures cart-wheeled over them; bubbles bounced in, distribution numbers spun inside them; arrows zipped around, market shares twirled around them. The whole thing was like a circus. A Power-Point circus.

I turned to look at The CEO's face. He looked dazzled. He was watching Pretty Boy with wide-eyed wonder as if he were a magician who had just materialized through the floorboards in a puff of smoke. Wimp-eater looked equally mesmerized, as if Christmas and his birthday had suddenly occurred on the same day. I squirmed with contempt. I wanted to squall at them that the only reason Pretty Boy's slides looked like sequences from The Matrix was because his company had a whole team of minions that specialized in making such charts. All Pretty Boy had done was feed the data into them.

'Excuse me,' a voice pierced the magic bubble. Everyone reluctantly tore their eyes away from Pretty Boy's slide to the source of that voice. Right Hand Man. He was stroking his chin thoughtfully, a frown creasing his forehead. 'That distribution number on the slide does not look correct,' he said slowly. I sat up in my chair. *Right Hand Man had actually managed to pin down one of those spinning numbers, long enough to realize it didn't look correct?* Woweee. I gazed at him with newfound respect.

'Well, this was the data that I was given,' I suddenly heard

Pretty Boy say. My head jerked towards him. He was looking at me pointedly. I quickly swept my sight around the room only to see all ten pairs of eyes trained on me. Embarrassed and confused, I wriggled in my seat.

'Did you give him those numbers?' Wimp-eater asked me menacingly.

My chair creaked. 'Err...yes,' I confessed. How had I screwed up again? God, I really was on a roll. But wait a minute, I thought; hadn't I shared exactly the same figures with Pretty Boy that the branch managers had sent to me?

'Well, they don't look correct,' Wimp-eater growled. He looked disgruntled, and impatient, as if he was itching to get back to front-row viewing of Power-Point Circus—Act 1.

'I'll have them checked S-sir,' I said. Wimp-eater's eyes bore into mine while a vein leaped out on his temple. Next to him, The CEO was frowning at me and shaking his head. I flushed red and felt completely exposed.

'May I continue?' Pretty Boy asked calmly. I glared at him and hoped lightening would strike him dead.

When Pretty Boy had finally finished, the whole room burst into wild applause. Both Wimp-eater and The CEO bounded up to congratulate him. Wimp-eater looked like he wanted to garland him and The CEO as though he would love to adopt him. Pretty Boy beamed at them both, his chest swelling further with pride. That it hadn't burst already was a wonder. Some minutes later, after all the (nauseating) backslapping and high-fiving was over, everyone started trailing out of the conference room. I was halfway to my desk, when I heard Wimp-eater holler from behind, 'Zoey! Come into my cabin. Right now!'

I froze for a second, then made a u-turn and dashed after him like a frightened puppy.

'Sit!' he instructed, his expression stony.

I sat down in the chair facing him.

Wimp-eater ran restless fingers through his hair, a sign I had come to recognize as one of imminent explosion. I prudently leaned back in my chair, and counted to 5.

One...Two...Three...Four...Five...

And boom!

'How could you be so careless?' he thundered. 'Sharing inaccurate data with that boy? It's completely unacceptable...(Wimp-eater's moustache was twitching, so was the rest of him—I wondered if that meant he was about to explode into flames)...Did you see the CEO's face? Did you *see* it? He was not happy. NOT HAPPY! I'm not happy either! Can't you do one thing right?'

Now, at that moment, what I should have said to Wimp-eater was: 'Look Mister...you don't scare me, okay?...and FYI, I didn't share inaccurate data...I am pretty damn sure that I supplied the same data that was sent to me by the branches...So quit making me the scapegoat, you big bully...And if you and The CEO are not happy, then, well, that is just TOUGH LUCK!' All that said, before blowing the nozzle of my imaginary gun and sauntering away into the sunset.

Instead, I uttered something exceptionally inane like: 'Erm, er...S-sir...'

Wimp-eater cut me off impatiently, 'You can't afford to be careless. Especially now that a month on, you will be up for employee confirmation.' He gave me a millisecond to absorb this piece of news before rushing ahead, 'And, as part of the confirmation process, you will have to make a presentation; a one-hour presentation on the gaps in our distribution, basis, all the market mapping data that you have been collating. More importantly, you will have to make this presentation to...(he paused for effect)...the CEO.'

Presentation to The CEO? **Presentation to The CEO???**

I sat there, face drained of colour, mind numb with terror, heart seconds from a cardiac arrest.

Wimp-eater leaned forward, his eyes piercing through my head. 'Now listen Zoey, and listen carefully. You will get confirmed only if you make a...a...what-you-call-it...' (he paused, mentally searching for a word, and eureka!) '...KICKASS presentation.' Looking mighty pleased with himself for his verbal prowess, he continued, 'It's very critical that you make a good impression on the CEO *this time*? Understood?' The emphasis on the words *this time* was not lost on me. I nodded stupidly and looked up. *Should I shoot myself now or later?*

When this talk got over, I tottered out of the cabin and toppled into my chair. All thoughts of the unfair accusation of my having shared inaccurate data had flown right out of my head. The only thing that now seemed to occupy it was the daunting prospect of making a presentation to The CEO, an hour-long one at that. How on earth was I going to do it? Sliver of dignity be damned, I thought. I should quit right now, because, let's face it, chances of my getting confirmed were about as slim as George Clooney getting married. I was about to write a frantic email to Lara, when my eye caught Pretty Boy hurrying across the floor towards my cubicle. Great, now what did he want?

'What do you want?' I questioned sharply, when he reached my desk. I didn't bother to look up.

'Um, Zoey,' he began, thrusting his hands into his pockets, 'I didn't mean to throw you under the bus in there...' he paused, shifted his weight from one foot to another, 'It's just that, well, you *had* shared that data with me...'

I took a deep breath, felt sudden tears sting my eyes. It appeared that Emotional Outburst was just around the corner.

'...and well,' Pretty Boy continued, 'that data was inaccurate...'

Ding Dong. Emotional Outburst had arrived; suddenly, all the pent up anger of the last few months...all the angst that had been building up inside of me...all the frustration that had been eating up my insides...all of it came gushing out in one barely coherent outburst.

'Yes. It's all my fault, right?' I half-yelled. 'It can't be yours. You with all your special sodding effects. Oh no, it's all MY fault...Never mind that that data was given to me by the branches...Never mind that all I had done was collate it...because it's all MY fault...all MY *bleeding fault*...(I was poking my chest with my thumb at this point)...because I am the good-for-nothing Management Trainee...the incompetent fool...the...the...'

'I don't think you are incompetent at all...' Pretty Boy broke in softly.

'...I may as well just get fired...I may as well...*what?* Not incompetent? Yes, you're darn right I'm not incompetent...But everyone seems to think so and now thanks to you The CEO is even more pissed off with me than before...(people were beginning to turn around and look but I didn't care. I was BEYOND caring)...and now I have to make this presentation... to him...on...on market mapping and what not...and...and...I am terrified...I might not get confirmed...I'll get fired...'

I paused to catch my breath. 'You'll do fine,' Pretty Boy broke in again, this time more firmly. 'No need to panic. Just breathe.'

I blinked, opened my mouth to speak again but before

I could, he added soothingly, 'And if you need any help…
(he paused for a fraction of a second, his eyes settling on mine
with unnerving steadiness)…any help at all, just let me
know.'

I stared at him, the wind sucked out of me. *Was that
'concern' in his eyes? No, of course not. Can't be.*

I wiped my dribbling nose; then mouthed a grumpy 'No
thanks,' followed by a prim 'I can manage on my own.'

Pretty Boy gave a tight nod, then turned on his heel and
walked away.

I frowned at his retreating back with suspicion. What was he
being so nice for, all of a sudden? Guilty conscience, I'll bet.
Well, I hope he chokes on it. I grabbed my bottle of water,
drained it down, then turned to my laptop and resumed typing.

From: Zoey Verma <zoey.verma@see-mail.com>
To: Lara Krishnan <lara.krishnan@see-mail.com>
Date: February 3, 11:28 AM
Subject: Screwed

Have to make a presentation to The CEO. And a good impression.
Else might get fired. Or not confirmed. Or both. So screwed. It's all
Pretty Boy's fault. He threw me under the bus. His words, not mine.
Hate him.

....

From: Lara Krishnan <lara.krishnan@see-mail.com>
To: Zoey Verma <zoey.verma@see-mail.com>
Date: February 3, 11:46 AM
Subject: Re: Screwed

Excuse me? But who the hell is Pretty Boy?

....

From: Zoey Verma <zoey.verma@see-mail.com>
To: Lara Krishnan <lara.krishnan@see-mail.com>
Date: February 3, 11:53 AM
Subject: Re: Re: Screwed

Hello? Did you not read? Have to make a presentation to The CEO. The CEO!!! Shitting bricks the size of Brazil. What am I going to do?

....

From: Lara Krishnan <lara.krishnan@see-mail.com>
To: Zoey Verma <zoey.verma@see-mail.com>
Date: February 3, 11:59 AM
Subject: Re: Re: Re Screwed

You have a pretty boy in your office and you didn't tell me????
Shame on you!!!
I want details. RIGHT NOW.
P.S: Is he tall? Does he have big feet?

....

In other news, that night when Velcro Man called up, I asked him for tips on how to make a good presentation. (Velcro Man had been quite a brilliant orator back in B-School days. Very Obama-like. I was sure he would have some brilliant tips/words of wisdom for me.)

And he did. They were as follows:

Velcro Man's Brilliant Words of Wisdom on How to Make a Good Presentation:
Words of Wisdom #1: *'God, you're an MBA...you should be comfortable making presentations by now...'*
Words of Wisdom # 2: *'Seriously, how hard can it be to make a presentation?'*
Words of Wisdom #3: *'I mean, there are bigger things to worry about than some presentation...'*

Luckily for me, Velcro Man also spent sufficient time enlightening me on The Bigger Things To Worry About Than Some Presentation. These were as follows:

1. That Certain Legendary Batsman had been on his 99th 99 for the past five overs.
2. That Certain Home Delivered Pizza was beginning to taste less like pizza and more like cardboard.
3. That Certain Diet Cola Drink, while low on calories (allegedly), tasted no better than pee.

Suffice it to say, Velcro Man's brilliant words of wisdom proved to be of no help whatsoever.

A week later, I had barely made any progress on my presentation. I had managed to put together just about five slides—all of which were CRAP, none KICKASS. Worse still, it was a Friday evening and instead of spending it in the company of my TV remote as I had hoped to, I was saddled with the prospect of the one thing I had come to dread the most—The Office Dinner Party. Why? Because they were big, fat, colossal bores. Perhaps, the only thing that made them slightly redeemable was the watching of a bunch of grown men making a mad scramble to some restaurant. Further, seeing them trample at least half a dozen people along the way, to sit in chairs closest to The CEO's table, so as to have the full advantage of currying his favour.

I was just contemplating crying sick and giving the whole circus a miss, when Right Hand Man lobbed up in my cubicle. 'We are all leaving in half an hour for the restaurant. Do you want a lift?'

'Erm, actually,' I mumbled, quickly assuming the expression

of someone about to collapse. 'I'm not feeling too well…' I quivered in my chair and began massaging my forehead to boot. 'My head is splitting…I think I'm going to be sick…'

Right Hand Man wasn't impressed. 'Have a Crocin,' he said unfeelingly. 'You can't miss the dinner. Not if you want to upset The CEO.'

'But he won't even notice my absence,' I protested, 'I am just a trainee.'

'He notices everything,' Right Hand Man said ominously. 'Miss the dinner at your own peril.'

God, I thought, as I watched Right Hand Man walk off. He made it sound as if we were all on Big Boss.

Sure enough, in a while, I found myself grumpily contemplating the innards of the restaurant. There was one long table booked for us, and The CEO had already taken his place at its head. Fully intending to noiselessly fade into the background, I rushed to a chair in the corner of the other end of the table. It was only once I had lowered myself into it that I noticed the person sitting opposite me. Pretty Boy. Damn. I stiffened in my chair, feeling suddenly like a cat perched on a tree, with no way down and no way home.

'Hi,' Pretty Boy said.

'Hi,' I responded.

A long pause of the awkward kind followed. I began fidgeting with my table napkin. 'How is your presentation coming along?' Pretty Boy finally asked.

'Fine,' I replied stiltedly, still fidgeting with my napkin.

Another long awkward pause. I shifted in my chair uncomfortably. I hadn't spoken to Pretty Boy since my Grand Emotional Outburst. Feeling suddenly sheepish about the whole event, and wanting suddenly to clear the air, I dropped the napkin on my lap and said, 'I'm sorry I, um, lashed out at you the other day...'

'That's alright,' Pretty Boy eagerly cut in. 'You were clearly...' (he took a moment to search for a word) '...*stressed*.'

I smiled feebly at him.

Awkward Pause No.3 followed. Pretty Boy broke it with, 'You can relax, you know. I promise not to pester you for any data tonight.' He was smiling, his eyes crinkling at the corners.

I stared at his eyes, my tummy performing a little flip. It just wasn't fair. Pretty Boy looked even prettier when he smiled. Not that it had any effect on me, I told myself. Pretty Boy's smile did not move me one bit. Not one damn bit. My tummy pointedly did another flip, leaving me feeling a little breathless.

Dropping my gaze, I spread the napkin on my lap and uttered a distracted, 'Right.'

Pretty Boy shrugged, then turned to the person sitting next to him (someone from the Marketing division). For the next few minutes, he continued talking to him. I let out an inward sigh of relief. For some reason, Pretty Boy made me uncomfortable. With all his prettiness and his laughing eyes. Really, he was most annoying.

I looked at my watch. 8.10 p.m. God. Another hundred minutes of this. I slid down my chair. I should have just gone home. I would have been in bed right now, watching re-runs of The Big Bang Theory instead of twiddling my thumbs here. Idly glancing at the table next to me, I saw the waiter serve two glasses of what looked like chilled Margaritas. I licked my lips and eyed them thirstily.

'You seem lost in thought,' I heard Pretty Boy say. 'Do I need to send a sniffer dog and a search party to pull you out?'

'No, just alcohol,' I blurted before I could think, then quickly checked back on Pretty Boy.

One corner of his mouth was curved up in a smile. Beckoning a waiter, he asked me what I would like to drink. Soon, the waiter arrived with a bottle of white wine. I lunged for my glass as soon as he had filled it and took a deep glug. I watched Pretty Boy swirl the wine in his glass, before taking a whiff. I scowled at him. Pretentious oaf, I thought, taking another deep slug from my glass purposefully.

I was already half way down my drink when Pretty Boy finally took his first sip. 'Good stuff, right?' he questioned, inspecting his wine. Jeez. Who did he think he was? Some World Renowned Wine Connoisseur cum Sommelier?

'I wouldn't know. It's all ethyl alcohol to me,' I snapped, downing another swill.

Pretty Boy's lips twitched. Speaking loudly enough for my ears alone, he leaned over and ventured, 'Is it me you don't like or is it office parties in general?'

'Um,' I floundered, temporarily thrown by his directness.

Pretty Boy's face grew suddenly serious. 'I'm really sorry that you got pulled up the other day for that data point on my chart,' he said. 'I didn't mean to get you into trouble.'

He looked so sincere, that I was dumbfounded, and managed to croak a 'that's all right'.

He waited for a moment, then holding my gaze, said softly, 'You didn't answer my question.'

'What question?' I asked daftly, feeling suddenly winded and out of depth.

'Is it me or is it office dinners in general?' he repeated, eyes still holding mine.

I felt a sudden urge to knock back some more wine. 'It's not you…' I said, lifting my glass to my lips (well maybe it was, but I could hardly tell him that. I mean, even I could not be that rude). I took a sip, then rushed on, 'I suppose I'm being poor company. You see, I'm not feeling too well. I should have gone home.'

'Oh,' he frowned in concern. 'In that case, are you sure having wine is a good idea?'

'Of course,' I nodded, suddenly alert and nabbing my glass as if he was going to snatch it away.

Pretty Boy eyed me with amusement. 'I guess it doesn't help that these office dinners are such a bore,' he said pleasantly.

I took another deep swill. I had by now downed nearly all of my wine. My insides were beginning to feel all warm and happy. Good ol' alcohol, I thought gazing at my wine glass affectionately. Thanks to it, I was suddenly feeling very benevolent. In fact, I was in a fair way to forgiving Pretty Boy for being a pretentious oaf. I flashed him a big smile. He blinked, looking blinded for a second.

'You are right,' I whispered, my voice beginning to slur. 'They are a blasted bore. I've already attended three of these since I've joined J&K, and I'm surprised I haven't slipped into a permanent coma already.' Picking up my glass, I drained the rest of my wine in one fell swoop. I was, soon, onto my second glass. Twenty minutes later, I was pouring my heart out to Pretty Boy about exactly how I had ended up in J&K.

'Do you know what the HR woman asked me?' I said, slapping my glass on my table with a loud clink. 'She asked me which animal I identify with…'

'Really,' Pretty Boy said, his lips tightening at the corners to suppress a grin. 'And which animal *do you* identify with?'

'Tiger, of course,' I announced, deciding that I may as well make a complete fool of myself, since I was already more than halfway there.

'You? A tiger?' Pretty Boy openly laughed.

I folded my arms, looking offended. 'Why can't I be a tiger?'

'Um, you just don't seem the type.'

'Why? What type do you think I am?' Before he could get a word in, I held up my palm and said, 'no, whatever you say, do not say Chihuahua!'

'Chihuahua?' Pretty boy said softly, trying not to choke on his chicken lollipop.

I took another gulp of my wine. It sloshed on the table as I put the glass down.

'You might want to go easy on that,' Pretty Boy suggested, his eyes on my glass.

I tried to focus on his face. 'I can hold my drink, you know,' I said primly, before letting out a loud hiccup.

Pretty Boy shook his head in amused tolerance.

'I have a confession to make,' I said impetuously, leaning forward, 'I'm not really a tiger, you know...I had Glasses-n-Whiskers fooled...'

'Glasses-n-Whiskers?' Pretty Boy echoed, clearly in the dark.

'That HR woman,' I said, frowning at Pretty Boy, 'Haven't you been listening? You really need to keep up.'

'My apologies,' Pretty Boy said wryly.

'Anyway,' I continued as if he had not spoken, 'I had Glasses-n-Whiskers completely fooled. Now, if I were on the panel, no one would be able to fool me...'

'Really?' Pretty Boy drawled softly, inclining his head, 'Let's put that claim to the test, shall we?'

I blinked at him, confused.

Pointing to Wimp-eater, he said, 'Him. What's his animal type?'

Comprehension dawned on me. I squinted at Wimp-eater.

'A blood, a blood...' I began, then homing in on the potato wedges on the tray left behind by the waiter, '...hound,' I finished absently, reaching for the tray.

Pretty Boy's eyes twinkled. 'And him?' he queried, pointing to Right Hand Man.

I turned around to look at Right Hand Man's face. 'Poodle,' I said, regarding him compassionately, 'a poodle trying hard to be a blood hound.'

'Very perceptive,' Pretty Boy said, looking impressed. He paused for a moment, then murmured softly, 'And what about me?'

'You?' I blinked, munching my potato.

He nodded, his eyes fastened onto mine. 'Yes...me...what am I?'

'Well,' I said, pausing, feeling suddenly flustered.

'She hesitates,' Pretty Boy murmured, leaning closer. I gaped at him, bewildered. *Was he flirting with me? Of course not. Couldn't be.* Blown, I looked away, my blurry eyes suddenly locking with Shiny-Faced-Trainee No. 1's. She was seated precisely two chairs away from The CEO (Big Surprise). Throwing a quick glance at Pretty Boy, she then looked back at me with a hardness that would pulverize granite.

'Well,' I said distractedly, returning Shiny-Faced-Trainee No. 1's stare, 'I don't know about you, but your *girlfriend*, there...' I was now wiggling my finger in Shiny-Faced-Trainee No. 1's direction.

'Girlfriend?' Pretty Boy interrupted.

My head pivoted around to him. The abruptness of the movement made me dizzy. I swayed back against my chair, hanging on to the table. Pretty Boy was now looking in the direction of my still-wiggling finger.

Girlfriend? Damn. Had I said that aloud? Me and my loose, alcohol soaked tongue.

At least I had been stopped from voicing the rest of that statement, which went something like, *your girlfriend is a first class bitch*.

Taking in Shiny-Faced-Trainee No. 1, Pretty Boy's expression cleared. 'She is not my girlfriend,' he said, turning back to me. He sounded almost offended.

'Right,' I said airily, picking up my fork. 'None of my business really,' I announced, waving my fork all about. It really wasn't. My business, that is. Never mind the fact that I suddenly felt enormously pleased.

'I don't have a girlfriend,' he said firmly. 'I am not seeing anyone at the moment.'

'Right,' I said again, giving him my best version of a nonchalant shrug.

'What about you?' he asked.

'What about me?' I echoed blankly, sticking my fork into the nearest tray.

'Are you seeing anyone?' he asked in a hushed tone. I looked up, muddled, from the piece of chicken tikka that had attached itself to my fork, to find him staring at me intently.

I closed my eyes and hiccupped. Velcro Man's face flashed before my eyes. I vaguely found myself wondering what animal type he was. Leech? Parasite? Feeling suddenly depressed, I slouched in my chair. 'Yes,' I said, opening my eyes...another hiccup...'Yes, I am.'

Pretty Boy leaned back abruptly in his chair. 'Right,' he said stiffly, with a shrug that vaguely resembled mine. At some point in the next few minutes, somewhere between the roasted chicken and the tiramisu, he turned to the person on his right again, and for the remainder of the meal, remained enthralled in his company.

'I'm a drunken fool,' I told Coolio, as I tottered into my kitchen about an hour and a half later. Coolio gave me an affirmative whir. 'Oh, bugger off,' I moaned, before stomping off to my room.

For the next few days, I worked on my presentation like a woman possessed, well into the night, during weekdays, and often right through the weekends. The day arrived when Wimp-eater demanded to see my presentation. Apprehensive and skittish as hell, I sat in his cabin, heart trembling, voice hoarse with terror. I had barely clicked on the second slide and uttered two words when Wimp-eater held up a silencing hand, 'The structure of this presentation is all wrong,' he carped, 'This is not how you should begin...' What followed was a word by word, slide by slide tearing apart of my presentation, until I no longer knew what in damnation it was all about.

Approximately an eternity later, I walked out of Wimp-eater's cabin, feeling like I had been run over by a train. Somehow, I managed to make my way to the washroom and latch the door, before flinging myself on the floor and drowning in my tears.

And in all that time, I tried to think of all the reasons why dying at the age of twenty-three was really not such a bad thing.

In the week that followed (during which time I ran Wimp-eater through my presentation, *all of seven times*) I remained a train wreck. Back in B-School, I had often cringed at the umpteen assignments, the long hours and the inhuman deadlines, but compared to the HELL that I was going through right now, B-School now seemed like a piece of cake.

Each time I showed Wimp-eater my presentation, he would change his mind about its flow. Each time I would run to my desk, restructure it and run back to him, only to have him change his mind again. 'Why can't he just make up his goddamn mind?' I bawled into the phone one day to Lara.

'Look on the bright side,' she replied, 'At least you are not grovelling on all fours trying to push some dowdy fridge down the throat of some dealer.'

Three more iterations later, Wimp-eater was still not happy. 'It's still not up to the mark,' he fussed. 'The font size on this slide does not look right...the colour scheme on that slide is not eye-catching enough...' He shook his head, and stroked his moustache a couple of times for comfort. 'Why can't you make your presentation more like that boy's?' (By that boy, he meant Pretty Boy, of course). I closed my eyes in frustration and took a deep breath. Only just before this, I had been informed that my presentation to The CEO which wasn't up for another week, had now been shifted to the following morning due to some change in The CEO's travel itinerary. I was already panicking and Wimp-eater's nit-picking wasn't helping one bit. Worse still, with all the changes I still had to make, and with the presentation on tomorrow, there was no way I would be able to make it for Chemical Curls' birthday party that night.

I messaged her as soon as I stumbled out of Wimp-eater's cabin. She called me immediately, 'You can't come??!! But Zoey, it's my birthday! And you're the co-host!!!'

'I know,' I apologized. 'Am really sorry, but my presentation has now been shifted to tomorrow, and I still have loads of work to do. You go ahead with the party. I'll stay over at my aunt's tonight.'

'Are you sure?' she fretted 'Why don't you drop in for a short while at least? You need a break…you've been working like crazy.' I hesitated for a moment. I was tempted. I mean, if there was ever a time in my life, when I desperately needed a drink, this was it. But alas, I couldn't drink, because I was a responsible adult and responsible adults simply did not get plastered on the night before a big presentation.

'I can't,' I finally said, deflated. 'Like I said, I still have loads of work to do.'

'Hmm. Should I shift the party to another evening then?'

'No,' I insisted immediately. 'You've been planning it for weeks. Please go on without me. And down a few shots on my behalf.'

'You betcha. But I hope you change your mind…'

Three hours later, (three hours spent slaving until I couldn't see clearly anymore), I did change my mind. I had had enough. I couldn't work on the presentation anymore. I had done all I could. No more. What I needed now was something medicinal to soothe my frayed nerves. Morphine was a strong contender; but alcohol (of the kind likely to be flowing at the party) won the race hands down. Never mind the fact that less than two weeks ago (on the night of the office dinner), I had taken a pledge (with Coolio as witness) that I would go without alcohol for a whole month at the very least.

Oh God, the office dinner party. Just thinking of it made me shudder. Since that evening, Pretty Boy and I had barely spoken. On the two occasions that we had, it was because he had needed some data. On both those occasions, he had been perfectly polite and utterly professional, making no reference, whatsoever, to that evening. Not that I was complaining. I had hiccupped and slurred through three glasses of wine, called every other J&K employee some kind of animal and nearly accused him of having a flagship bitch of a girlfriend. I was more than happy to play amnesia. Truly. Except that every now and again, Pretty Boy's warm, crinkling eyes would swim into my head. And at the most unexpected of times too. Like today, when I was being yelled at by Wimp-eater…ping…Pretty Boy's face, warm, crinkling eyes and all. And the other day, when I was playing Angry Birds on Chemical Curls' IPad…ping…Pretty Boy's face again. Out of nowhere. Mocking me. Really, it was most annoying.

Anyway, I thought, no-alcohol-for-a-month pledges be damned. Tonight I desperately needed a drink. Dammit, after all the hard work, I jolly well deserved it. Seizing my bag, I packed up my laptop and walked out.

I had just stepped out of the elevator into the lobby when I saw a figure lounging near the gate, cigarette in hand. My heart inexplicably pounded in my chest. Even from a distance, I could tell it was Pretty Boy. As soon as he saw me, he dropped his cigarette to the ground, quickly stubbing it out. 'I'm trying to quit,' he said, almost guiltily, as I neared him.

For a change, it was my turn to be amused. 'I see,' I said evenly. 'And how's that working out for you?'

'Not too well, obviously,' he shrugged ruefully, running a hand through his hair.

I smiled. A pause followed. I was about to fill it with a, *bye, see you tomorrow* when he cleared his throat. 'Presentation done?'

I shook my head, then let out a long breath. 'I don't know about the presentation, but *I* am definitely done. Can't work on it anymore.'

He nodded, as if seeming to understand. 'You'll do fine,' he said encouragingly. 'Don't worry.'

I shunted from one foot to another, for some reason feeling unaccountably shy. 'Any tips for me from the Power Point Genius?' I managed to ask.

He frowned, appearing thoughtful. 'Yeah, one actually,' he said eventually, his face breaking into a lopsided smile. 'Dazzle them with special sodding effects.'

When I let myself into my apartment, a little later, the party was on in full swing. A sea of somewhat familiar faces stood around, wolfing booze and swinging to music. I looked around for Chemical Curls and spotted her canoodling with her boyfriend in a corner.

'Oh cut it out, you two,' I said, striding over and shamelessly interrupting them.

'You came!' Chemical Curls sang, disentangling herself from The Boyfriend, who tugged at his shirt sheepishly, and coughed. 'Yay! I'm so glad,' she squealed, giving me a high-five and a bear-hug.

I grinned. 'I'm just here for a bit though. Just a couple of drinks to get the edge off.'

'Yep, yep,' she nodded, then turned to her boyfriend and batting her eyelids, purred, 'Get a beer for my co-host, please?'

Chemical Curls' boyfriend was a shy, nerdy and slightly dorky looking piece, who, at that moment, was gazing at her with a desperate hangdog look. 'Coming right up!' he said eagerly, before disappearing into the crowd.

Three hours and ten yards of beer later, I was still at the party. I had gone from 'Have a few drinks to take the edge off' to 'Get sloshed so as not to live to see the next day.' And I was feeling absolutely delighted about it. On a chair in a corner of the hall, I sat jogging my head to Justin Timberlake and sipping a gigantic LIT in drunken splendour (yes, I was now mixing my drinks too). A gangly, long-haired, dopey-looking fellow broke out of the crowd and ambled towards me. I squinted at him as he flopped into the chair next to mine, then watched him pull out a cigarette from his pocket, light it and take a long, slow, orgasmic drag. Then, cigarette dangling between his fingers, he started bobbing his head to J.T. Suddenly, the distinct, familiar smell of grass assailed my nose.

I let out a giggle. '*Ganja*, huh?'

He turned to me, eyes glazed. 'Shhh,' he hissed, 'It ain't *ganja*, dude. It's called vitamin G.'

I let out another giggle.

'Want a drag?' he drawled.

'Nah,' I hiccupped, then jabbed my head with my pinky finger. 'Gives me headache.'

'Tough,' he croaked. He was now swaying in his chair, zooming in and out of focus. He was making me giddy.

I squeezed my eyes shut. 'Not that I don't have one already,' I squeaked. Dopehead didn't respond. I opened my eyes and glanced at him sideways. He had fallen to his side, eyes closed, mouth open. I shrugged, lifted my glass and took another large swipe.

A deep groan suddenly escaped from him. 'Aaaarrrrrgggghhhhh…'

I tuned in to him in slow motion. His eyes were now half open. 'Dude, this music sucks man,' he moaned, 'What is this shit? Eh? What is this crap…'

I blinked at him. *Excuse me? Hic. Had Dopehead here just insulted my taste in music? Hic. Had he just insulted the Great J.T?*

'...Gotta tell the host of this party man...to play some trance...trance, dude...it's the best shit...it f&%ing transports your mind, man...it's awesome...it...'

I sat still, trance-like. It had occurred to my woozy brain to ask myself the question 'Just who the fuck was this bloke?' He sure as hell didn't look familiar.

'Do you even know who the hosht of this party ish?' I slurred.

'Some chick man,' he mumbled. 'I'm just the friend of the friend of...' He stopped short, having realized that he couldn't be bothered to finish that sentence because his joint needed attending to. This time he took such a deep drag, that I thought he would burst a lung.

'I'm Jimi by the way,' he said dopily, a moment later. 'Jimi, with an I. As in Jimi Hendrix.'

'I'm drrrrunk,' I announced to no one in particular. 'Drrunk with a D as in D...U...N...K...'

'Dunk?'

'Eh?'

'Dunk?'

'Who?'

'D-U-N-K? Dunk?'

'D-U-N-K. Drrrrrrrunk.'

'Right on.' Dopehead drawled. He was sticking his thumb up.

'Yep, don't plan to (hic) be alive tomorrow.'

'Right on,' he gurgled again.

I took another noisy slurp of my LIT. I was beginning to feel sick. Good, death couldn't be far off.

'Aaaah...dude, I am so stoned,' Dopehead groaned. He was clutching his head, eyes closed.

I nodded sympathetically; then devoured the rest of my LIT in one long gargle. Buaaaaarrrrrrr, I let out a loud burp.

Dopehead's eyes flew open.

He was looking at me mesmerized. 'Right on,' I heard him echo, before I sank into my chair and passed out.

★

I woke up the next morning to the sound of Chemical Curls' stilettos and two unfortunate realizations:

Realization 1: That I was still alive to see that morning.

Realization 2: That I was still alive to see that morning, through bleary eyes in a pounding head.

'You really drank last night, woman.' Chemical Curls was beside my bed, poking me with a manicured finger.

'Whaaa? Who's that?' I wheezed, burying my head under the pillow.

'Your room-mate, you idiot.'

'Oh,' I croaked, lifting my pillow an inch. 'What time is it?'

'8,' she said, suspending over me.

'Whhaaa?' I sputtered, then screwed up my eyes at the clock on my table. It *was* 8. Crapola, I was late! I must have slept through the alarm. And my presentation! It was less than two and a half hours away! I jolted up on my bed, held my head tight. It felt like a boulder. Ten men were sitting on it and banging it with sledgehammers. Oh God, I was never going to drink again. *Ever.*

'You need a hot shower,' Chemical Curls said, pushing down my bed cover.

Yep. Hot shower. Superb idea. But how to go about it? Ah good, I was being pulled up by Chemical Curls. She was tugging at my hand and pushing me into the bathroom.

A hot shower (one that I could have gladly stood under forever), a quick change of clothes (which left me feeling dizzy all over again), and a few burnt toasts later, I managed to leave for work. Sixty minutes later, I tramped into office, hangover still in attendance. Wimp-eater almost immediately opened his cabin door and marched out towards me, Right Hand Man gliding around his right hand.

'You!' he yelled, snapping his finger at me. 'Presentation with CEO at 11.30 a.m. sharp.' Then he twirled around, Right Hand Man now at his heels, re-entered his cabin and swung the door shut. Owww. Now to the thrumming in my skull, I could add ringing. I pressed down on my head with both hands. I was so screwed. So *so* screwed. *God, why had I drunk so much last night? Why? Why? Why?* I was still clutching my head when Pretty Boy leaned over the wall of my cubicle.

'Hi,' he said cheerfully.

I glanced up, my eyes groggy.

'Hi,' I croaked, then bit my lip. My stomach was beginning to churn.

'Rough night?' Pretty Boy asked, with interest.

'I think I might be half drunk,' I explained, then winced mentally. God, what must he think? First I quaff wine like it's water during an office dinner party and then I walk into office hung-over on the day of my presentation. He must think I'm a first rate drunkard.

'Ah,' he said, his eyes creasing with amusement. 'First Aid might have some pills for that,' he added solemnly.

'I'm going to need surgery, not pills,' I muttered. Cripes. Why did I suddenly care what Pretty Boy thought of me.

Pretty Boy flashed a broad grin. I stared at him, my breath sticking in my throat. Dammit. Why was he so devastatingly pretty?

'Don't you have something to do?' I asked, churlish, suddenly feeling annoyed. 'Like making colourful excel formats?'

'Are you shooing me off?' he queried, deliberately leaning over my cubicle.

'Yes,' I said, feeling sick, my stomach heaving again.

'Why?' he asked, amused, 'Are you going to have another meltdown?'

'Worse,' I mumbled, clapping a hand over my mouth. I was about to throw up. Hell and Damnation. I pushed my chair back, signed off with a sort of grunt and dashed to the washroom as fast as my headache would allow.

Quite a while later, just as I was coming out of the loo looking like the walking dead, I nearly head-butted into Shiny-Faced-Trainee No. 1 (who, for some reason, was looking shinier than usual). 'Oh hi, how did your presentation go?' she crooned. I peered at her face. It was literally aglow. Why, I wondered. Was it because of Pretty Boy? Was he the reason for her Xtra Glow? Had they begun secretly dating? The thought left me feeling twitchy all over.

'Not over yet.' I said through gritted teeth, 'It's at 11.30.'

'Are you okay?' she asked suddenly, tilting her head, 'You don't look so good.'

'I'm fine,' I said, then hastened to change the subject, 'How did *your* presentation go?'

She beamed, as if she had been waiting for me to ask that question. 'It was great! The CEO was really impressed. In fact…' she paused, patting her hair down '…he told me that my confirmation was a sure thing.'

So that's why she was glowing. Hmmph. 'Good for you,' I said woodenly.

'Yes! And guess what, he also told me that I was a strong contender for a fast track promotion.'

I tried not to be sick again. 'Great. Um, well, anyway, I have to go...'

'Yes, right. All the best for your presentation.'

I cranked up a brittle smile, then hobbled over to my desk, picking up a coffee along the way. Of course, Shiny-Faced-Trainee No. 1 was getting confirmed. Of course she was being promoted in the not too distant future. Of course. Bet she had dazzled The CEO with all her Intelligent Questions. All nine thousand, seven hundred and eighty-two of them.

Another wave of nausea pummelled me and I plonked heavily on my desk. Eyes closed, my mind neatly summarized my actions of the previous evening.

- Drank on an empty stomach. Tick
- Had more than three drinks. Tick.
- Mixed drinks. Tick. (Beer. Vodka. Rum. Tequila. Tick. Tick. Tick. Tick.)
- Got slaughtered on the eve of Big Presentation. Tick.
- And last, but definitely not least: Nearly threw up on Pretty Boy. Big Fat Tick.

Eeeks. Seriously. What the *hell* had I been thinking? At least Pretty Boy was nowhere to be seen now. Thank God. The last thing I needed was he having a laugh off me.

But my presentation? What was I going to do about my goddamn presentation? I could barely speak, let alone *present*. I took a few deep breaths, then began praying. *Please God, please set off a 9.5 Richter scale earthquake just below where I'm sitting right now. A Tsunami would be fine too. Anything to have the presentation not happen.* Unfortunately, God couldn't have been bothered, because 11.29 a.m. arrived without the slightest whiff of a natural disaster. At exactly 11.30 a.m. The CEO's secretary called up, 'The CEO is expecting you in his office.'

'Right,' I croaked, slapping my now empty coffee cup on the table; then I got up and began walking the long walk from my desk to The CEO's cabin, attempting to gather my courage along the way. It's not as if he is Count Dracula, I told myself. Or Godzilla. I gave a nervous hoot of laughter. I can do this, I thought, wiping my sweaty palm against my trousers. 'I CAN do this,' I told myself, feeling the rise of another attack of Projectile Vomit.

I reached the cabin door all too soon, took a deep, shuddering breath; then knocked. 'May I come in, Sir?' I said, voice all a-quiver. 'Yes,' The CEO shouted from within. I opened the door and entered. The CEO sat at his table, facing Wimp-eater; the two of them were in the midst of a discussion. I stood, trembling, near the door and cleared my throat. They both looked up.

'Yes, come in Zoey,' The CEO said, sitting back in his chair. At this point, I felt weak. I had just had a creepy vision of The CEO pouncing for my head and biting it off mid-way through my presentation. Please God, I prayed in my mind, if you can't cause an earthquake, at least let me expire right here. No such luck. Five seconds later, I was still alive and quaking in my shoes.

The CEO ran an appraising look over me, then grinned mockingly. 'Let's see what she has to say,' he winked at Wimp-eater, who in turn shrugged and began restlessly tapping his foot.

I inched forward and stuck my pen drive into the laptop on the table. Seconds later, hands fumbling, I clicked on Full Screen, then braced myself for what I knew would be the worst hour of my life.

11

I'm not quite sure whether my presentation went well or not. All I know is that after having been haunted by repeated images of The CEO rushing for my head and biting it off, I was quite surprised to walk out of his cabin an hour later, with my head still intact. I mean, sure, there had been one butt-clenching moment during that hour when The CEO had flailed his arm about, and I had thought that he was diving for my head. But, phew, no—he had just been making sure that that rebellious hair tuft was still wrapped firmly around his balding skull.

'So how did it go?' Lara asked, twenty minutes after I was out of The CEO's cabin.

'I'm not sure,' I mumbled into the phone.

'Not sure? What do you mean not sure?'

'Well,' I whispered, moving out of earshot of Shiny-Faced-Trainee No. 1 who, for some reason, was rather shiftily hanging around my desk. 'He just nodded at the end of my presentation, grunted an "OK" and then dismissed me. So I'm not sure what that means.'

'Hmm,' Lara said thoughtfully, 'I suppose that means that it wasn't a complete disaster.'

'You think?' I asked, chewing my lip.

'Yep. Positive. He probably would have bitten your head off if he hadn't been happy.'

'That's what I thought too,' I replied happily.

'What about that chick from marketing? How did her presentation go?'

'You mean, Shiny-Faced-Trainee No. 1? Well, get this, she was told by The CEO that not only was she definitely getting confirmed but that she was also likely to get a promotion soon.'

Lara sniggered. 'Why am I not surprised?'

'I know. Seriously. Anyway, what about you? When is your presentation to your boss?'

'Well, actually, I have some news.'

'What news?' I asked distractedly. I could see Shiny-Faced-Trainee No. 1 still loitering. Was she trying to eavesdrop on my conversation? Trying to figure out how my presentation had gone? I cast her a tetchy look. She stared at her phone, pretending to look busy. Very suspicious behaviour. I twirled around, and like a demon, plodded to the far end of the floor.

'I'm putting in my papers,' I heard Lara say.

I froze mid-plod. 'You are what???' I squawked.

'You heard me,' she replied calmly.

'Lara,' I cried, before realizing that everyone was turning to look at me. I dropped my voice, 'I know things are bad, but do you really want to quit without a job in hand?'

'I do have a job in hand, silly.'

'*You do?*'

'Yep,' she sang, 'It's an Equity Finance Company. The role is perfect for me. And the pay is good too!'

'Oh.'

'And guess what,' she continued happily, 'The job's in Mumbai! I'll be there within a month!'

'Well, that's great,' I said, recovering. 'I'm really happy for you. Erm, really. And plus you'll be coming to Mumbai. So, um, yay.'

I was happy for Lara. Truly. I was happy that she was getting out of that hostile dump in Chennai. I was happy that she would be in Mumbai by the end of next month. And most of all I was happy that she was finally going to do something that she had wanted to do all along. But even as I congratulated her, I knew that somewhere wrapped up in those feelings of happiness there was a pang...no, make that several pangs...of envy. I was going to lose my one and only ally-in-angst to a job that she was going to love. For some reason, that stung.

That night, when Velcro Man called up, I told him about my presentation.

'So it wasn't a complete disaster,' he said and before I could reply, proceeded to drop a bomb on my lap. 'I'm planning to come down to Mumbai for the weekend.'

I felt my heart sink. 'You're coming down to Mumbai for the weekend?' I dimly repeated.

'Well yeah, this whole long-distance relationship thing sucks.'

I sat down heavily on my chair. It was one thing for Velcro Man to whine down the phone. He couldn't see me and so I could do other chores while he whined, such as, you know, dust my room, paint my toe nails, cook myself some noodles, watch an episode of Modern Family...But to whine face-to-face? And that too for forty-eight hours at a stretch (give or take a few)? That was *way* more than what my system was equipped to handle.

Without warning (as was customary) the image of Pretty Boy hopped in to my head. Only this time, it was an image of Pretty Boy *and me*...more precisely, me jumping on him, kissing him wildly. Hey. Hey. *Hey.* Now where the hell had that image come from? I couldn't possibly *like* Pretty Boy. Could I? No, of course I couldn't. My heart tilted on its axis, then gave an enthusiastic kick. 'Oh shut up,' I mentally said. 'I do not like Pretty Boy. I have a boyfriend. And besides Pretty Boy doesn't even like me. He probably thinks I'm a drunken loser.' The thought left me feeling strangely depressed.

'You don't sound too thrilled,' I heard Velcro Man say.

'No, no. I *am* thrilled,' I lied, pushing back a lump of panic. 'I'm, erm, positively ecstatic.'

Velcro Man hmmmed, before going on to do what he did best. This time the subject was: The Inconvenience of Long-Distance Relationships.

'So when are you planning to come down?' I asked (exactly 56 minutes later, when he finished whining and when I had adequately recovered from The Bomb That Had Been Dropped On My Lap).

'I can fly down next-to-next weekend,' he immediately replied, before proceeding to drop Bomb No. 2 on my lap: that I foot half his air-fare, because apparently it was only fair that I did. (This, despite the fact that I was near-broke due to my gigantic dental bills and that he had a job that paid him double of what mine did.) I now had a new nick-name for Velcro Man — The Grinch.

'*He asked you to foot his air-fare?*' Chemical Curls exclaimed in a shrill voice, when I finished narrating my conversation with Velcro Man over dinner.

'Well half of it,' I clarified, taking a bite of pizza.

'*But you are practically broke!*' Chemical Curls was still shrieking. '*You have all those dental bills to pay! You can't foot his air-fare!*'

'Yeah, I told him that,' I mumbled, my mouth full.

'Hmmph. You know what, if he is planning to stay here, you should charge him lodging fare. That'll teach him. Better yet, you should dump him. He sounds like a douche.'

'He's not that bad,' I said, trying to force down the pizza, 'just a bit whiny and a bit clingy and well, a bit Grinch-like...'

Chemical Curls glared at me. 'YOU SHOULD DUMP HIM.'

'Okay okay,' I whispered, startled by her sudden ferocity.

That night I thrashed about in bed, brooding over the Velcro Man issue. I had to dump him. I knew I had to, but I just couldn't appear to get around to doing it. Maybe because having a crutch of any kind, especially one that was familiar, was better than having no crutch at all; Velcro Man was my crutch. In fact, he was the human equivalent of a cigarette. He did absolutely nothing for my well-being, but was a habit I couldn't easily kick off.

Perhaps somewhere out there was a Velcro Women Anonymous, I thought. If so, I really ought to try signing up for it.

The next morning, eyes *slitty* with sleep and mind still preoccupied by the Velcro Man situation, I walked wearily into the office lobby. I had just pushed the elevator button, when Pretty Boy materialized by my side. My heart kicked again. (It seemed to do so every time Pretty Boy surfaced in my immediate vicinity, not to mention in my head. Really, it was most inconvenient.)

'Hi,' I heard Pretty Boy say.

Suddenly remembering my make-out fantasy from the day before, I made a strange noise that was somewhere between 'Good' and 'Morning'.

He peered at my face. 'Not hung-over *again*, are you?' he asked. The special emphasis on 'again' was not lost on me.

'Of course not,' I replied primly, throwing him a foul look. God. He really did think I was a drunken sod.

Pretty Boy shook his head, laughing softly. 'You are so easy to rile,' he said, his shoulders shaking. I stared at him for a second, then jabbed his arm like a silly teenager, before dissolving into a smile.

'Anyway, I hear congratulations are in order,' he said.

'For what?' I asked, frowning. The elevator doors slid open. I followed him into it.

'For nailing your presentation, of course' he said, pressing the third floor button.

My eyes widened. 'Who told you I nailed my presentation?'

Pretty Boy shrugged. 'Well, if you hadn't, the CEO wouldn't have told your boss to share it with me.'

'He said that?' I asked excitedly.

'Yep. He said that you had done a good job on it and that I should have a look at it.'

'Those were his exact words?' I asked, trying not to sound too keen.

He laughed. 'Yes! Those were his exact words.'

I looked down at my shoes, smiling uncontrollably, 'Well, I don't know if I did a good job. I think I did okay.'

'You did a good job,' Pretty Boy repeated.

I glanced up, my smile stretching from ear to ear.

'Especially for someone who was hung-overed beyond repair,' he teased.

I wrinkled my nose at him and grinned bashfully.

There was a moment of silence. 'So, the boyfriend and you are going to celebrate tonight, huh?' Pretty Boy asked softly. He looked suddenly serious, his eyes staring into mine. I felt weak, felt my smile waver.

The elevator doors began to slide open.

He continued staring at me for a moment. 'Well, actually,

he…' I began. Before I could finish, he cut in with an abrupt, 'I've got to go. I have a meeting. Enjoy yourselves.' Then he got out of the elevator swiftly, swung me a backward wave and walked away.

I stepped out staring after him, feeling bemused by his sudden change of mood. Then I shook my head and reminded myself of The CEO's words about my presentation. I had done a good job, he had said. I had done a *good* job. As the words sunk in, I hugged myself, let out a loud whoop, then hopped aboard Cloud 9.

In the days that followed, things at work took a sweeping turn for the better. Wimp-eater now deigned to talk to me directly instead of via Right Hand Man; Right Hand Man, in his place, had now begun treating me as Fellow Employee instead of Lowly Minion, and even The CEO had stopped shooting me looks of the 'Grrr-you-incompetent-fool' variety.

In other news, Pretty Boy had been extremely busy (and largely out of my range of vision). Word had it that his project was coming to an end, and as a parting gift to J&K, he was neck-deep in making some Brilliant Earth Shattering presentation that would forever swing its fortunes. Unlike the last time, however, this time I was quite looking forward to watching him present—for reasons, I wasn't entirely sure were—erm—professional.

When the day of the presentation arrived, we all gathered in the conference room. The CEO began the session with an introduction on how, while we now had a strategy in place for our overall network expansion, we still needed to have a firm marketing strategy too. 'Our consultant will now take us through his ideas. Please pay attention, *everyone*.' He turned to Pretty Boy and beamed. Pretty Boy stood up, smiled prettily at everyone (my heart fluttered as if on cue), then opened his mouth and began. Everyone leaned forward to catch every little gem that flowed out of his mouth. Everyone, including me.

One slide through his presentation, he paused dramatically. Then he announced, 'Your fridge is fuddy-duddy,' he said. 'It needs a makeover.' Everyone gasped in shock. Our fridge? Fuddy-duddy? How dare Pretty Boy speaketh such words? But Pretty Boy had spoketh those words; and luckily for him, The CEO was nodding his head in agreement as if they were the words of The Prophet. I gaped at Pretty Boy in awe, then whirled back to The CEO. The CEO seemed to like the words 'fuddy-duddy'. He was savouring them on his tongue. 'No more fuddy-duddy!' he crashed his fist on the table and declared, 'I want fridge with a fashion sense.'

Everyone slowly began bobbing their heads. I too joined them in the head-bobbing. Because of course, our fridges were a bunch of fuddy-duddys. Anyone could have told them that (anyone with guts that is). I looked at Pretty Boy with renewed awe, then found myself thinking about Coolio. Poor Coolio, I thought, nibbling my pen guiltily. Poor Fuddy-Duddy Little Coolio.

'Everyone, let's brainstorm,' The CEO roared. Everyone nodded, rolled up their sleeves and began thinking hard on 'How To Make Our Fridge Fuddy-Duddy-Free'. Soon everyone began raining suggestions, left right and centre. I sat confounded in a corner, trying to keep up. But when, even after over an hour, suggestions continued to pour in with levels of animation rising higher and higher, my ears began to wonder whether it was indeed a fridge that was being discussed and not a time-travel machine. I gave up taking notes and began doodling Coolio on my pad, instead. *Losers*, I thought, shaking my head. *Boy, do they need to get a life.*

Some minutes later, stifling a yawn, I began checking my office emails on my laptop. A new mail sat in my inbox—a mail from Pretty Boy. Sent a minute ago. With a subject line that read:

Is that a fridge you are doodling?

I caught a side-view glimpse of Pretty Boy. He was deep in the throes of a discussion with the marketing team, spiritedly spouting ground-breaking ideas it appeared. I scowled. God, he was SO one of THEM. 'Of course not!!!!!' I typed back, exclamations marks and all, then immediately resumed adding the final touches to my doodle—a cute, little, butterfly-shaped magnet on Coolio.

I was still doodling when my pen froze mid-air. I had just had an epiphany. The truth that had been swimming in the bowels of my brain had suddenly torn through to hit my forehead like lightening. *'It's not they who are the problem, silly. It's you,'* the Voice of Epiphany explained: *'You don't belong here. You are the misfit. Do you really want to dedicate your whole life to a fridge? A fuddy-duddy one at that?'*

In slow motion, I placed my pen down. Holy Moley, I thought. Voice of Epiphany had a point. If anyone was a misfit in this scenario, it was me. I was the one who didn't belong; who had never belonged. I had been trying to fit myself into this job, ever since I had joined, had been cussed in the process, all to what end? Did I really want to dedicate my whole life to a fridge? And yes, a fuddy-duddy one at that?

I glanced again at Pretty Boy. He was still deep in discussion. He was in his element, as if 'consulting' was what he was born to do.

My fingers flew over my keyboard. You really enjoy what you do, don't you? I typed, then pressed send.

Pretty Boy checked his mail a minute later. His reply was almost instant.

For the most part, yes. Don't you?

I shook my head, then looked up. An air of determination settled on me. The way forward was suddenly clear to me in a manner that it had never been before. For the first time in—at a rough estimate—23 years and 11 months, I knew exactly what I had to do.

Later, when the 'brainstorming' session was over, I trotted off to my cubicle. Collaring my chair, I hurriedly clicked on a folder on my desktop, opened a document and hit Print. Then I sprinted over to the printer, collected the document and breezed over to Right Hand Man. 'Boss in his cabin?' I asked.

Right Hand Man nodded. His head was buried in some file.

'Anyone with him?'

Right Hand Man shook his head, then paused, looking up, 'He did mention that he wanted to have a word with you some time today.'

'Oh. Did he say what about?'

Right Hand Man shrugged.

'I'll punch in to his cabin right away then.'

Right Hand Man nodded, then turned back to his file.

And so, with print-out in hand, I knocked at Wimp-eater's cabin.

'Come in,' he yelled.

It had been almost six months since I had been in the Mumbai Head Office and in all that time I was quite sure that I had walked through Wimp-eater's cabin door at least a hundred times. One would have thought that my heart should have gotten used to it by now, but clearly it hadn't. Each time, it drummed and thwacked, like a heavy metal band. Today, as it turned out, was no different.

I took a deep breath, opened the door and walked in. Wimp-eater looked up from his laptop. 'Sir,' I said, above the din of my heart, 'I wanted to discuss something with you.'

'Ah, good you've come,' Wimp-eater said, leaning back in his chair. 'I wanted to have a word with you myself. Have a seat.' I swooped down on a chair. Wimp-eater opened his drawer, scrabbled its contents and fished out an envelope.

'Here you go,' he said, leaning forward to thrust it into my hand.

'What is it?' I asked, curious.

'Open it,' he commanded.

I quickly tore the envelope open and read the contents of the letter. *'Dear Zoey...yadda yadda yadda...we are pleased to inform you...yadda yadda...your employment has been confirmed...yadda yadda...woah...*

Employment confirmed? My eyes darted to Wimp-eater's face which had softened into a smile. Wimp-eater had never smiled at me like this before. I sat gaping at him, dumbstruck.

'Congratulations,' he said, clasping his hands on the table. 'You are now a confirmed J&K employee.'

I blinked, then looked down. *I had been confirmed? Wimp-eater thought that I was J&K Employee Material?* For a few seconds I felt woozy with pleasure, then I remembered the purpose of my visit. I stared at the resignation letter in my hand, suddenly plagued by a series of second thoughts. *Should I put in my papers? Was I being too impulsive? Should I sleep over it? What will everyone say?*

'The CEO was quite happy with your presentation on Network Gaps,' Wimp-eater was now saying. 'Keep this up and you will soon be promoted to Manager...'

I stared at him, my mind drawing up a quick list.

Reasons for not putting in my papers:

1. Have achieved much-coveted Confirmed Employee Status,
2. Am once again being regarded as Star Trainee With Bright Future,
3. Additionally, am also being regarded as Promotion-worthy, *plus*
4. Mom very likely to throw Great Grand Mother of All Fits if I do put in my papers;
   and also,
5. Do not have another job in hand, hence will have to go paycheck-less for a while (highly inconvenient this, given looming dental bills and growing addiction to paycheck).

'Also Zoey,' Wimp-eater broke into my thoughts, 'I think you are now ready to handle a territory, you are ready to sell fridges...'

Reasons for putting in my papers:

1. Will have to Sell Fridges

'Sir,' I broke in, mind made up, 'I really appreciate this, Sir, but I came in to hand this to you...' I leaned forward and placed my letter on the table.

Wimp-eater picked it up, flicked a glance across it, then put it down with exaggerated precision.

'You are putting in your papers?' he asked, disbelieving.

I nodded. 'Yes, Sir, I am.'

Wimp-eater picked up the printout again and stared at it. Chastened by his softened stance towards me, I was suddenly very glad that I had ditched Drafts 2 and 3 of my resignation letters for the more professional Draft 1.

'Are you sure about this?' he asked, still staring at it.

Suddenly I hesitated, thrown back by a scary vision of my mom angrily slapping me around with heavily buttered parathas; then managed to recover, 'Yes, Sir. I am.'

Wimp-eater glanced up, considered me for a few seconds, then—burst forth, 'But why? Why would you want to quit at this point? Just when you are getting confirmed...'

The Truth? Because I had finally taken the leap of imagination to realize that before I tried growing a thicker skin, I needed to get comfortable in my own.

'Because Sir, sales is just not my cup of tea,' I said instead, deciding that this wasn't a movie, and therefore I was not required to hit him with some dramatic and wholly inane dialogue.

Wimp-eater shook his head in disbelief. 'Then why the hell did you join this company?' he half-yelled. Hmmm. Perhaps, I *should* have hit him with some dramatic and wholly inane dialogue.

Too late now. I shrugged and smiled feebly. 'I don't know what to say, Sir, except, thank you for the opportunity.'

In a short while, feeling slightly overwhelmed, somewhat scared, but a whole lot lighter and happier, I walked out of Wimp-eater's cabin. Just one more thing left to do now before the proverbial free fall. I walked over to my table, picked up my phone, sifted through 'Contacts,' and pressed 'Velcro Man'.

Epilogue

It has been six months since I quit J&K. In the days that followed, reactions to my 'Moment of Madness' were manifold.

First, there was Lara. *'How could you quit without a job in hand?!! That's career suicide! How will that look on your CV?!*

Then, there was Chemical Curls, *'You've quit? Without a job? Does that mean that I'm going to have to hunt for a new roomie?'*

And then there was my mom, *'What??? Left your job? Hai Bhagwaan! But why? Do you think good jobs grow on trees? First, you don't want to meet any good boys...then you say bye-bye to good job...It's all my fault. All MY fault...I gave you too much freedom...TOO MUCH freedom...'*

Dad had been the only one who hadn't cared to demonstrate the range of his vocal chords. He had simply nodded, shrugged his shoulders and gone back to reading his newspaper. Dad, and Coolio of course—who had whirred me to the comfort of watermelon ice cream (family pack).

To the relief of everyone, however—three months later, I did manage to find a job. Officially, my designation reads 'Assistant Manager—Talent Acquisition'. Unofficially, I am referred to as 'that HR woman'. My job in a nutshell? Visiting B-Schools, interviewing prospective candidates and recruiting 'talent'. (No, I don't bombard unsuspecting interviewees with questions like 'Which animal do you think you are?' But, I do have my own way of sifting the Poodles from the Tigers, and the Poodles Who Have The Potential To Be Tigers.)

Is it my Grand Calling in Life? I don't know. But what I do know is that I no longer wait in slow agony for the clock to inch towards 5.30 p.m.; I am no longer choked with dread at the prospect of going to work on a Monday morning...and best of all, when posed with the question, 'Do you enjoy what you do?' I am happy to say that I can truthfully answer it with a, 'For the most part, yes.'

P.S. Post driving home the message (in person, over the phone, via text and on Post-its), Velcro Man finally decided to unglue himself.

P.P.S. Following that, post another month of heart kicks, flips and somersaults, Pretty Boy finally decided to ask me out on a date.